"Does B▮▮▮▮▮▮▮▮▮▮▮ Me

Jesse said, a sardonic smile curving one corner of his sexy mouth.

"No," Mandy lied. "Though I wondered why you chose this place for us to meet."

"But this is where it all began, Mandy. This is where our son was conceived. It's the perfect place to discuss his future."

He nodded toward the center of the grassy, moonlit glen. "I'd wait for you right there while you slipped out of your father's house to meet your half-breed lover."

Tears filled Mandy's eyes. *Oh, please, Jesse,* she cried silently. *Don't do this.*

But Jesse wasn't through with her yet. He took a step closer, hooked a finger in the strand of hair that shadowed her face and dropped his lips to her neck.

Heat curled through her. "What do you want from me?" she whispered.

"My son."

Dear Reader,

Silhouette Desire is proud to launch three brand-new, emotional and romantic miniseries this month! We've got twin sisters switching places, sexy men who rise above their pasts and a ranching family marrying off their Texas daughters.

Along with our spectacular new miniseries, we're bringing you Anne McAllister's latest novel in her bestselling CODE OF THE WEST series, July's MAN OF THE MONTH selection, *The Cowboy Crashes a Wedding*. Next, a shy, no-frills librarian leads a fairy-tale life when she masquerades as her twin sister in Barbara McMahon's *Cinderella Twin*, book one of her IDENTICAL TWINS! duet. In *Seducing the Proper Miss Miller* by Anne Marie Winston, the town's black sheep and the minister's daughter cause a scandal with their sudden wedding.

Sexy Western author Peggy Moreland invites readers to get to know the McCloud sisters and the irresistible men who court them—don't miss the first TEXAS BRIDES book, *The Rancher's Spittin' Image*. And a millionaire bachelor discovers his secret heir in *The Tycoon's Son* by talented author Shawna Delacorte. A gorgeous loner is keeping quiet about *His Most Scandalous Secret* in the first book in Susan Crosby's THE LONE WOLVES miniseries.

So get to know the friends and families in Silhouette Desire's hottest new miniseries—and watch for more of their love stories in months to come!

Regards,

Melissa Senate

Melissa Senate
Senior Editor
Silhouette Books

Please address questions and book requests to:
Silhouette Reader Service
U.S.: 3010 Walden Ave., P.O. Box 1325, Buffalo, NY 14269
Canadian: P.O. Box 609, Fort Erie, Ont. L2A 5X3

PEGGY MORELAND
THE RANCHER'S SPITTIN' IMAGE

SILHOUETTE *Desire*®
Published by Silhouette Books
America's Publisher of Contemporary Romance

SILHOUETTE BOOKS

ISBN 0-373-76156-2

THE RANCHER'S SPITTIN' IMAGE

PEGGY MORELAND

published her first romance with Silhouette in 1989. She's a natural storyteller with a sense of humor that will tickle your fancy, and Peggy's goal is to write a story that readers will remember long after the last page is turned. Winner of the 1992 National Reader's Choice Award, and a 1994 RITA Award finalist, Peggy frequently appears on bestseller lists around the country. A native Texan, she and her family live in Round Rock, Texas.

To my Georgetown girlfriends, better known
as the WADY Birds: Kathy Craig, Cindy Davies,
Lali Ewan, Pam Fling, Susan Hoyt, Becky Kennedy and
Libby Wood. Thanks for welcoming me into the nest and
allowing me the opportunity to "fly" with you.

Prologue

Under the shadow of darkness and with only the moon's silvery light to guide their movements, the young lovers rose from the rumpled blanket as one. Perspiration beaded their bodies in the sultry night air like an early morning dew, yet they clung to each other, replete but reluctant to let the other go.

They sighed and drew an arm's length apart, looking deeply into each other's eyes. Scents of crushed grass and wildflowers tangled with the headier scent of sex and filled their senses, making leaving that much more difficult.

Even though he was aware of the danger in lingering, Jesse dipped his head over Mandy's again for one last kiss. "You need to go," he whispered.

"I know," she murmured. But the taste of him was wild and intoxicating and filled with enough of the forbidden that Mandy was reluctant to leave him. She splayed her fingers across the breadth of his chest and watched his eyes darken. The quickening of his heart beneath her palm brought a temptress smile to her swollen lips. "But maybe just a minute longer," she suggested.

Her breath against his mouth was as tantalizingly sweet as the fingers that roamed his chest. Jesse caught her hands in his and drew them to his lips, wanting her again, as desperately as he had only moments before, but knowing they'd already stayed too long. "It's too chancy, Mandy," he warned. "At any moment someone might find you gone and come looking for you. If they found us—"

Mandy quickly pressed her lips to his, silencing him, not wanting to hear the dangers of their secret meetings voiced aloud. "They won't," she promised and dipped quickly to pick up her panties and bra. With shaking fingers she quickly donned them.

On a sigh, Jesse followed her lead, pulling on first his jeans, then his shirt, then dropping down on the blanket to tug on his socks and boots. But his eyes never left Mandy, watching as she frantically pushed buttons through holes in her blouse and shimmied into her jeans.

"Mandy," he said, his slight Mexican accent caressing each syllable of her name as he reached for her hand. "My heart aches at the thought of leaving you."

The poetry in him never ceased to amaze her and her blood warmed and thickened with her love for him. With a quivering smile, she threaded her fingers through his and braced herself as he used her weight to pull himself to his feet. Stepping nearer, she wrapped her arms around his waist and pressed her cheek against his chest.

"I—I'll miss you," she whispered brokenly, the lump in her throat making voicing the words difficult.

"No more than I'll miss you," he returned, squeezing her tightly against him. "When can we meet again?"

She lifted her face to his, wanting to take with her the memory of his handsome face, the love that glowed so vibrantly in his dark eyes. "Saturday. Daddy is going to San Antonio to a sale and won't be back until Sunday, late."

His brow furrowed. "But how will you slip away unnoticed?"

In the moonlight, her smile radiated confidence. "Don't worry. I'll think of a way."

The sound of a dry twig snapping came from the protective arc of trees that surrounded their secluded spot. Jesse stiffened, his fingertips digging into Mandy's neck as he pressed her face to his shoulder to stifle her cry of alarm. He cocked his head, listening, searching the perimeter for the source of the sound, praying that it was only an animal moving through the thick stand of trees on its nightly hunt for food. But as his gaze struck a bright sheen of polished metal gleaming in a beam of moonlight, he knew it wasn't an animal he'd heard. It was something much worse, someone much more menacing.

He quickly shifted, placing himself between Mandy and the barrel of the rifle aimed at them. Even as he did, a man stepped from the shadows of the trees and into the moonlight. The rifle was braced against his wide shoulder, its barrel aimed at Jesse's chest.

"Jesse Barrister!"

Jesse heard Mandy's sharp intake of breath, felt her fingers claw at his back as the roar of her father's voice filled the night. Defiantly Jesse lifted his chin, meeting the angry gaze of Lucas McCloud.

"What do you want, McCloud?" he demanded.

"What's mine." With a snarl, Lucas took a step closer and waved the barrel of the gun. "Mandy! Get out from behind him, or I swear I'll blow a hole clean through the both of you."

The cold-blooded threat pushed ice through Jesse's veins. "You'd kill your own daughter?"

"I'd rather see her dead than teamed with the likes of you. Now get out from behind him, Mandy."

When Mandy shifted as if to obey the order, Jesse thrust his arms behind him to hold her in place. In doing so, he offered Lucas an even broader target for his aim. "You're not on McCloud land," he warned Lucas, "you're on Barrister land. You don't give the orders here. I do."

Lucas barked a laugh, but kept the gun aimed dead on Jesse's chest. "You bastard," he spat out. "You don't give orders here or anywhere. You're nothing but the whelp of Wade's Mexican whore."

Jesse felt his blood heat at the insult. Not for himself. He'd long ago grown accustomed to the word bastard. But no one had the right to sully his mother's name. "Bastard or not, I'm a Barrister, and no McCloud is welcome on Barrister land."

Though Lucas's gaze remained locked on Jesse's, his words were for his daughter. "Did you hear that, Mandy?" he mocked. "No McCloud is welcome on Barrister land. And *you* are a McCloud."

"She's mine!" Jesse shot back before Mandy could answer. "And as soon as she's of age, her name will be Barrister, not McCloud."

The metallic grate of the rifle's lever being rammed

into firing position split the night in two. "Over my dead body," Lucas roared. "No daughter of mine will ever carry the name Barrister. I'll kill you first."

Mandy jerked free of Jesse and threw herself in front of him, placing herself between her father and the man she loved.

"No, Daddy, please," she sobbed. "I love Jesse."

Lucas's eyes narrowed, but he never lowered the rifle. Its barrel now pointed at the hollow at Mandy's throat. "Get away from him, or I swear I'll kill him for the thieving bastard that he is—and you right along with him."

Before Jesse could stop her, Mandy raced across the space that separated them from her father and grabbed for the barrel, shoving it high in the air. The gun went off, the sound of its explosive report bouncing off the trees and echoing in the dark glen.

Knocked off-balance by Mandy's attack, Lucas fell back a step, but quickly regained his footing, wrapping a thick muscled arm around Mandy's waist and pulling her hard against his side.

Jesse lunged forward, but Lucas quickly one-armed the rifle back into position, stopping him.

"Jesse, please," Mandy sobbed. "Go before he kills you."

Jesse glared at Lucas McCloud, the hate that burned in him mirrored in the older man's eyes. Slowly he shifted his gaze to Mandy's. Even more slowly he lifted a hand to her, his palm up in silent entreaty. "Come with me, Mandy. Come with me now. We can leave here, we can go somewhere where your father will never find us."

"I'll find you," Lucas warned, his voice low and threatening. "There's not a hole deep enough for you to crawl into where I can't find you. And when I do, I'll kill you.''

Mandy looked at Jesse through eyes blurred with tears, torn between her love for her father and the man who owned her heart. She knew her father would make good his promise. He hated all the Barristers; the feud between the two neighboring ranches had raged for four generations. But he hated Jesse most of all, not only because he was Wade Barrister's illegitimate son, but because Lucas could never see beyond the color of Jesse's skin or the Mexican accent that no amount of Americanization had been able to erase.

She knew she could find a way for them to be together. She just needed time to think, to formulate a plan. Even if it meant waiting the few months that stretched between this night and her eighteenth birthday before she saw him again, she knew her love for Jesse would survive the separation. Especially when the reward at the end was that they could be together forever.

Unable to stand the rawness of his expression, the love and expectancy that gleamed in his eyes, she dropped her gaze, praying that he would understand. ''No, Jesse. I can't.''

For a moment he seemed stunned by her response, then his body slowly stiffened and his hands closed into fists at his sides. With a savage cry, he lunged, his arms raised, his fingers curled as if already closing around the neck of the man who threatened his happiness, the man who stood between him and the woman he loved.

A shot rang out, deafening Mandy. She clapped her hands over her ears, her body throbbing with the rifle's report. The scene in front of her slipped into slow motion and she watched Jesse's eyes widen, his face twist in pain. The impact of the blast spun him to the left and she watched in silent horror as he staggered two steps, then crumpled to the ground.

Mandy's scream ruptured the night. ''Jesse! No-o-ooo!''

One

The three women stood, shoulders almost touching, staring up at the portrait of their father that had hung over the fireplace in the den of their family home for over twenty years. Pictured astride his horse, the aptly named Satan, Lucas McCloud seemed a man born to a saddle. The artist had captured him leaning forward slightly with his forearm braced casually atop the saddle horn and the bridle's leather reins gathered loosely in his opposite hand.

Set against a panorama of blue Texas sky and the rocky hills and green meadows that made up the Double-Cross Heart Ranch, both rider and horse appeared indomitable. One could almost feel the stallion's wildness captured by the artist's brush. Standing on a slab of limestone that jutted from a high ridge, with his ears cocked forward, his head held high, the horse met the viewer's gaze with an arrogance, a ripple of muscled strength, a compelling dominance that equaled that of the man on his back.

And no one was more aware of these traits than the three women who stood staring up at the portrait. They'd stood just so every year on this same date for eleven years, to mourn as well as honor the man pictured above them.

Yet anyone who saw them together would never dream the three were sisters, that they shared the same parents, the same pool of genes. The daughters of Lucas McCloud were as different in personality as they were in looks.

Mandy, the oldest, stood to the left of the portrait, her hands molded around a mug of steaming coffee. An almost fragile look disguised a deep inner strength and a will that matched that of the man who'd spawned her. Thick auburn hair brushed her slim shoulders, a testament to her femininity, while a denim work shirt and faded jeans, her standard wear, hid her soft curves. Her chin was tipped high, almost in defiance, with only the slight tremble in her lips giving her emotions away as she stared up at the painting of her father.

Samantha, or Sam as her family called her—a much more fitting name for the tomboy of the family—stood in the middle, the tips of her fingers tucked rigidly into the front pockets of her faded jeans. Raven-black hair, scraped back in a ponytail, hung almost to the middle of her back. Though tears burned behind her eyes, her lips remained pressed together, showing no emotion as she stared at the man who'd dominated her life until his death.

Merideth held the position at the right, her long graceful fingers wound negligently around a crystal wineglass. Taller than the others by two inches, Merideth was often mistaken as the oldest…but one look at the pouty lips, the bored expression, quickly gave away her position of honor as the baby of the family. Her sisters, the McCloud housekeeper and everyone else who came in contact with Merideth had succeeded in spoiling her rotten after her mother's untimely death in a car accident by giving in to her fits of temper, her unending demands. Lucas was the only one who'd had the grit to stand firm against her, refusing to give her what she truly wanted most…a one-way ticket away from the confines of the Double-Cross Heart Ranch.

With a sigh, Merideth turned away from the portrait, tucking a stray lock of blond hair behind her ear. "Well, I for one am glad he's gone."

Horrified, Mandy wheeled to stare at her. "Merideth!"

Merideth shrugged as she sank fluidly onto the leather sofa, drawing one slender foot beneath her. She pushed out her lower lip and jutted her chin in the famous pout that had earned her the nickname "the woman America most loves to hate" from *Soap Opera Digest*. "Well, it's the truth," she said disagreeably. "He was mean and domineering and controlled our lives until the day he died." She lifted her gaze, meeting Mandy's shocked one with one of defiance. "*You*, of all people, can attest to that."

Though her cheeks reddened with heat, Mandy tightened her grip on her mug and managed to keep her tone even. "He was our father," she returned. "He loved us—in his way. Besides," she added emphatically, "it was his wealth that enabled all of us to achieve our dreams. *You* should at least be grateful for that."

Merideth dipped her chin, peering at Mandy from

beneath one neatly arched brow. "*Our* dreams?" she repeated, drilling Mandy with a look that had sent stage directors and makeup artists alike running for cover.

"Back off, Merideth," Sam warned as she, too, turned away from the portrait.

"Oh, for heaven's sake!" she exclaimed in annoyance, shifting her gaze to Sam. "It's true and you know it. You were able to go to veterinary school, which Daddy would never have allowed if he'd lived, and I bought a ticket to New York and the means to live as high as I want while I do what I've always wanted to do, act. But what did Mandy get? Hmmm?" she quizzed pointedly as she turned to Mandy for an answer.

"I got the ranch," Mandy murmured, turning away.

"We *all* got the ranch," Merideth reminded her. "But you were the only one who wanted to continue to live here and run the place. What I want to know is what Daddy's wealth bought *you*. Was it able to buy you *your* dreams?"

Mandy felt the tension build in her back as Merideth's words stabbed into old wounds still unhealed. "I have the money. I've just never chosen to spend it...until now."

Merideth immediately sat up, dropping her foot to the floor and scooting to the edge of the sofa. "Now?" she repeated, then quickly shook her head, shoving out a hand to stop Mandy before she could reply. "Oh, puh-l-e-e-ease tell me you're not going to buy some new exotic breed of cattle to run, or build some new monstrosity of a barn on the Double-Cross?"

Mandy turned back, glancing first at Sam, then Merideth. "No. I'm going to buy the Circle Bar."

Merideth bolted to her feet while Sam's eyes widened in shock. Both women were more than familiar with the Circle Bar, the ranch that bordered their own, and with the feud that had raged between the two for four generations.

It was Sam who found her tongue first. "You're going to buy the Circle Bar? B-but why?" she stammered.

"Because I've heard that it might be for sale," Mandy replied, lifting her chin, praying her two sisters would leave it at that. But she should have known better. Merideth, especially, would never accept such a vague response.

"Reason enough if you had a need for it…which you don't." Merideth narrowed her eyes suspiciously. "So what's the real reason behind your interest in the Circle Bar? Do you think that it will bring Jes—"

"No!" Mandy all but shouted to keep Merideth from fully saying the name out loud. "I'm buying it for Jaime. He has a right to some portion of his heritage."

The quietest and at times the most softhearted of the three, Sam moved to Mandy's side, draping a sympathetic arm over her sister's shoulder. "Jaime doesn't need the Circle Bar," she comforted. "He's got you and the Double-Cross. He doesn't need anything from the Barristers."

Though she understood Sam's reasoning and appreciated the show of support, Mandy stepped from beneath her sister's arm, tightening her fingers around the ceramic mug. "I think he does…or will, at the very least. I can't give him his father, but I *can* give him a link with his past."

Merideth lifted her hands heavenward, then dropped them limply to her sides in frustration. "It's a good thing Daddy's gone because if he heard you talking such nonsense, he'd lock you in your room for the rest of your life!''

Mandy turned her eyes on Merideth, meeting her sister's gaze steadily. ''But that's just it. Daddy *is* gone. He can't stop me from doing what I want anymore.'' She set her mug on the desk, then rounded it, dropping onto the sofa next to Merideth. ''There've been rumors since Wade Barrister's death that the Circle Bar might be put up for sale. If anyone deserves to own it, Jaime does.''

''Whether that's true or not is irrelevant,'' Merideth argued. ''You know as well as I do that Margo Barrister would never sell the Circle Bar to a McCloud.''

A sly smile turned up the corner of Mandy's mouth. ''She'll never know until it's too late.''

Merideth reared back, looking at Mandy askance. ''And how in the world do you think you can buy the ranch without Margo being the wiser? After all, she *is* Wade's widow.''

''I've already thought all this out. I'm going to talk to my lawyer tomorrow. I'm going to request that he set up a dummy corporation, one that can't possibly be traced back to me. The corporation will buy the property, then, when Jaime's of age, I'll change the deed to his name. He'll have an inheritance of sorts. Something that no one can deny him.''

Merideth, who prided herself on her ability to work a situation to her favor, acknowledged Mandy's cleverness with a spattering of applause, then rubbed her palms together with glee. ''Margo will be furious!''

Mandy's smile broadened. ''Yes, she will, won't she?''

Merideth fell back against the sofa, hooting at the

ceiling. "Oh, I hope I'm there to see her face when she finds out the news. The old biddy. It'll serve her right for all her wicked ways."

Sam didn't accept the news with the same enthusiasm. She, too, crossed to the sofa and sank down next to Mandy, concern for her sister wrinkling her forehead. "Are you sure you know what you're doing? Sometimes it's best to let the past alone. You might be borrowing trouble if you go through with this. Margo won't take something like this lying down."

Mandy slipped her hand into Sam's and squeezed. "But it will be too late for her to do anything about it. The land will be mine by then. The damage will already be done."

Merideth sat up and stretched her hand across Mandy's lap to add hers to those of her sisters. "Well, I for one stand behind you. I may not agree with your reasons for buying the Circle Bar, but I certainly respect your right to do what you want with the money Daddy left you. In fact, I think it's rather like poetic justice, don't you?" She glanced up at the portrait of her father and smiled. "In fact, darling Daddy is probably turning over in his grave right now."

Mandy stepped from her lawyer's office and paused just outside the door. She released her pent-up breath in a long shuddery sigh. She'd done it. She'd set the wheels in motion. She'd signed all the papers required to set up the dummy corporation and she'd given her lawyer power of attorney to act on her behalf. Now the wait began.

She caught her lower lip between her teeth as the implications behind her actions set in. Had she done the right thing? she worried silently. Was she in fact borrowing trouble as Sam had suggested? She gave herself a firm shake and made herself take that first step toward the bank of elevators at the end of the long hall and the journey home to the Double-Cross.

No, she told herself firmly. Jaime deserved the Circle Bar. He'd been denied enough in his short life. He was due an inheritance, a part of his heritage denied by the illegitimacy of his birth.

Caught up in thoughts of the trouble that might lie ahead, Mandy unconsciously glanced up as the elevator dinged its arrival. She froze on that spot of carpet, a good thirty feet from the elevator door as she watched a man step through the opening. He turned immediately to the left without glancing her way...but not before she caught a glimpse of his face; of that strong profile shadowed by a black Stetson; of that quirk of mouth and long purposeful stride that defied anyone who was of a mind to challenge him.

Jesse.

Oh, God! she cried silently, tightening her hands into fists at her sides. What was he doing here? And why now?

His step slowed and his shoulders veered slightly as if he was going to turn. Mandy sucked in a sharp breath and quickly ducked down a hallway on her right. Flattening herself against the wall, she listened, holding her breath, but her heartbeat thrummed in her ears, drowning out all other sounds. She squeezed her eyes shut, praying that he would go on in the way he'd started and that she could escape unseen.

Hands hot and damp against the cool walls, she waited, listening, silently praying for what seemed like an eternity against the sound of his approach. Five minutes passed, each second like a silent bomb exploding within her head. Knowing she couldn't hide there forever, weak with fear, she eased down the wall and braved a quick look down the hall.

Empty.

She sagged back against the wall in relief. Then, with an effort, she pushed herself upright and ducked around the corner, running away from the elevator and toward the stairwell at the end of the hall.

Tearing down ten flights of stairs at high speed was nothing compared to her fear of exposure.

"You're sure it was him?"

Mandy whirled, flattening her hands on her father's desk, her green eyes wild as she met Merideth's doubtful look. "Yes, I'm sure! He stood less than thirty feet away."

Sam stepped behind the desk and looped an arm around Mandy's shoulders. "It could be only coincidental that he's returned," she murmured soothingly. "It may have nothing to do with Jaime at all."

"I don't care *why* he's back," Mandy wailed, refusing to be comforted. "I've got to protect my son."

Sam shared a look with Merideth, and Merideth came from the opposite side of the desk to tuck her hand through the bend at Mandy's elbow. For all her selfishness, Merideth was a McCloud and together she and Sam, as they always had in the past, formed a solid wall of support around their sister. "He can't hurt Jaime, Mandy," she insisted, her voice filled with a conviction that Mandy didn't share. "We won't let him. Besides, Jesse doesn't even know he fathered a son."

Mandy lifted her head and turned tear-filled eyes to

Merideth. "But what if he finds out? What if he tries to take Jaime away from me?"

Merideth fought back a shudder, refusing to give in to the fear that Mandy's questions drew. She'd learned well from her father that a show of fear was a sign of weakness...and Merideth McCloud had used that lesson well, always displaying an impenetrable confidence that had served her well as she fought her way through the ranks of ambitious actors to capture one of the leading roles on a daytime soap opera.

Mandy had learned that lesson, too, but at the moment was too shaken to remember it. Merideth knew it was up to her to give her the slap she needed to remind her. "So what are you going to do?" she asked in disgust. She knew she sounded harsh, but in her mind, the situation called for it. "Just hand Jaime over to him without putting up a fight?"

Mandy whirled, her expression one of shock. "Of course not!"

"Then quit thinking about what *might* happen and focus on the facts. Jaime is *your* son. You gave birth to him, you raised him alone without help from Jesse or anyone else. Jesse had no place in his life other than planting a seed."

"But what if he takes me to court? What if he tries to establish his parental rights?"

Merideth tossed up her hands in frustration. "And what judge in the country would settle those rights on him?" She grabbed Mandy's hands and squeezed them between her own. "He's *your* son, Mandy. Not Jesse's."

Mandy clung to the lifeline Merideth offered. "I know that. I do. But if he finds out—?"

Merideth squeezed her hands, silencing her. "Come

back to New York with me. You and Jaime can stay
with me until the dust settles and we see what Jesse's
intentions are.''

Slowly Mandy squared her shoulders, pulling her
hands from Merideth's. ''No. That would be running
from trouble. And no McCloud ever runs from trouble.''

Tossing back her head, Merideth laughed, the me-
lodious sound filling what once had been Lucas
McCloud's office. ''That's my girl! I knew you had it
in you.''

Mandy frowned, eyeing Merideth suspiciously, realizing too late that Merideth's taunts were all an act
to make her sister see reason. ''You're a brat, you
know that, don't you?'' Mandy grumbled. ''You always were.''

Merideth fluffed her hair with a playful, self-satisfied
grin. ''That's what they tell me,'' she said proudly and
moved to flop down on the leather sofa that faced the
desk.

Mandy continued to frown at Merideth, but Merideth
merely folded her hands behind her head and preened,
proud of her accomplishment. She crossed her bare feet
at the ankles, wiggling toes painted a garish red before
adding, ''And don't worry. I'll stick around for a while
just in case you need reminding that you're a Mc-
Cloud.''

Mandy's brows shot up. ''You can't do that. You've
got to get back to New York and your job!''

Merideth lifted a shoulder in a careless shrug. ''It'll
be there when I get back,'' she replied, confident of
her importance to the soap opera she starred in.

''You don't need to stay,'' Sam interjected, stepping

forward to hook a hip on the corner of the desk. "I'll be here as backup if Mandy needs me."

Merideth arched a brow, turning her gaze on Sam. Slowly, her lips curved in a proud smile. "I'd forgotten that the newly graduated and highly competent Dr. Samantha McCloud was setting up her veterinary practice on the Double-Cross." She lifted her hands, diamonds glittering, and let them drop. "Well, then I guess my services aren't needed." She turned to Mandy. "You'll be in good hands with Sam to look out for you and I'm only a telephone call away." Lazily she stood, stretching her arms above her head with catlike grace before moving to gather her two sisters into a loose embrace. After hugging them both, she stepped back and thrust out a hand, palm up. "One for all and all for one," she challenged. "The Three Musketeers."

Laughing, Sam and Mandy each slapped a hand on top of Merideth's. "Always," they echoed in unison.

Jesse made the turn off the highway and passed below the wrought-iron archway that marked the entrance to the Circle Bar and headed for the house. The Big House. That was how the Barrister home was referred to by those who lived and worked on the Circle Bar.

Though he'd thought himself immune to the past, Jesse could feel the muscles of his stomach tightening while beads of sweat broke out on his upper lip. With a muttered curse of self-condemnation, he dragged his wrist beneath his nose and glared through the windshield at the road ahead. He took his foot off the accelerator and eased on the brake, bringing the truck to a stop at the crest of the hill that overlooked the valley.

Spotlighted by a brilliant summer sun, the two-story Georgian-style mansion below him looked as out of place as Jesse had always felt while living on the Circle Bar. Instead of the carefully groomed lawns with drooping magnolias and oaks heavy with moss that one would expect surrounding such a structure, the home was bordered by pastures of grazing Hereford cattle and hills covered with rock, cedar and cactus.

Margo Barrister might have lost the war when she'd failed to persuade Wade Barrister to move to Atlanta after their marriage more than forty years before, but she'd won a battle by haranguing him until he'd finally torn down the original Barrister homestead and replaced it with this monstrosity, a testament to Margo Barrister's roots in the more genteel south.

The thought of Margo pushed a scowl across Jesse's face. Mrs. Barrister. That's what she'd insisted that he call her. Not Mother—God forbid that she ever admit that he was Wade's son—not even Margo. She'd accept nothing less than impersonal formality from him.

Hate curled in his stomach like a doubled-up fist at the memory. He'd never called her "Mrs. Barrister" as she demanded. He'd never referred to her in any way at all. It had been easy enough to avoid, since she'd refused him entrance in her home from the day of his arrival on the Circle Bar.

His frown deepened as he remembered that day. Margo had screamed obscenities, ranted and raved when Wade had brought his fourteen-year-old bastard home with him. She had refused to allow Jesse even to cross the threshold, demanding instead that Wade take him to the bunkhouse to live with the wranglers who worked the Circle Bar. And that's exactly where Jesse had lived until the night he'd left the Circle Bar, and Texas, almost thirteen years before.

No, avoiding Margo had been easy.

But this confrontation, the one awaiting him in the valley below, he knew he couldn't avoid. Shaking off the unpleasant memories, he shifted back into gear, eased off the clutch and started downward to the Big House.

Through the gleaming windows of her formal living room, Margo caught a glimpse of a cloud of dust swirling over the hill. Stiffening, she slowly placed on the table the vase of flowers she'd just arranged and moved to peer out of the window. Pulling back the silk draperies, she craned for a better view.

"Damn," she swore under her breath. Though she didn't recognize the black truck that kicked up the cloud of dust, she knew who rode inside. Jesse. He was back to claim his inheritance.

Her lips quivered in silent rage. He was back to claim the Circle Bar. Wade had left her the house when he'd died, but not the land it stood on. He'd left that to the son of that Mexican whore of his! That Wade would dare to insult her so publicly, to flaunt his bastard child for all the world to see, to strip her of the very land, the dynasty that opened doors for her in Austin society, made her see red.

She placed a hand against her heart, forcing herself to take a deep calming breath. It wouldn't do for Jesse to read her disgust, her anger…her desperation. She needed him, whether she cared to admit it or not. She didn't know what his plans were. Not yet, at any rate. He had made no contact with her since Wade's lawyer had notified him of Wade's death and of his subsequent inheritance.

Would he sell the Circle Bar? she wondered fleetingly. Or would he move back and work the place himself as Wade had wanted? Her stomach convulsed. The very thought of having to watch that miserable bastard walk *her* land was too appalling even to consider. She hoped he planned to sell. If he did, she'd buy the land and the Barrister dynasty would go on, just as it had in the past, except with Margo at the helm.

But would he sell to her? she wondered as she monitored his approach. Her fingers curled into a fist at her side, her manicured nails cutting into the tender flesh of her palm as she watched the truck roll to a stop in front of her home.

Immediately, she forced her fingers to relax. She could handle Jesse Barrister. Hadn't she managed to manipulate Wade for years? She watched as Jesse stepped down from his truck and was struck anew by his resemblance to her dead husband. Wade had done this to her on purpose, she thought spitefully as Jesse stepped up onto the wide veranda and disappeared from her sight. He'd left his land to his bastard son as one last stab at Margo because of her inability to give him an heir.

The doorbell chimed and Margo forced her fingers to release the drapes. Inhaling deeply, she drew herself erect, smoothing her hands down the front of her linen skirt, then lifting them to run her thumbs beneath the open collar of her matching blouse, composing herself for the confrontation ahead. Moving silently across the thick Aubusson carpets, she made her way to the front door and opened it, forcing a smile to her face.

"Why, Jesse!" she exclaimed in her southern drawl, as if unaware of his arrival. "What a nice surprise! Please come in," she invited graciously, swinging the door wide.

* * *

Jesse Barrister was no fool. He recognized a wolf in sheep's clothing when he saw one. His expression never once wavered as he met Margo's gaze. "I can handle my business right here," he said tersely.

"Business?" she repeated as she stepped back into the opening she'd created. "What business?"

"My inheritance, to be exact." Jesse watched as she struggled to keep the false smile in place.

"You've seen Wade's lawyer, then?"

"I just left his office. He showed me the old man's will." Even now Jesse couldn't voice the man's name out loud.

"I know this must be difficult for you," she murmured sympathetically, "coming back after all these years. I know how unhappy you were here. If you like, I can purchase the land from you and free you of whatever responsibilities Wade has burdened you with and whatever obligations you might feel. That way you could get on with your life with the least bother."

Jesse eyed her suspiciously from beneath the shadow of his Stetson's brim. He didn't know what Margo was up to, but it certainly was no good. He knew her far too well. Although selling the land had been his plan when he'd left the lawyer's office, something made him hesitate.

"I don't know," he replied slowly. He turned and looked over his shoulder at the sprawling land, the grazing cattle, the distant hills, the corrals where he'd sweated and worked alongside the other wranglers.

He'd hated every minute of the time he'd spent on this ranch and had been reluctant to return. He'd thought to come here, tell Margo his plans, then get the hell out of town, leaving behind the past and all the bad memories tied to this place.

But now he wasn't so sure.

Slowly, he turned back to Margo. "I'll be staying here for a while. Just until I decide what I want to do with the place."

Margo stepped back, lifting her hand again in invitation. "Well, then you must stay here. I'll have Maria prepare a room for you."

Jesse snorted. "I don't think so. The bunkhouse suits me just fine."

"Oh, that's not necessary," Margo hurried to assure him. "You'll be much more comfortable in the Big House. Besides, I'm sure that's what Wade would have wanted."

"Would he?" Jesse's lips curled in a scowl. "Somehow I doubt that."

Margo struggled to think of something to say. "W-well, if you're sure…" She lifted a hand to point the way. "The bunkhouse is—"

Jesse turned his back on her, cutting her off. "I know the way."

Margo moved to the window and stood, her eyes narrowed, her lips pressed tightly together, and watched Jesse walk back to his truck. Tall, broad shouldered, that cocky swagger. She shuddered in revulsion at the sight. With the exception of the darker color of his skin, the slight Spanish accent, he could have easily been mistaken for Wade Barrister at the same age. And that alone was enough to draw Margo's ire.

She'd married Wade Barrister forty years before, blinded by his handsome face and awed by his wealth, thinking herself in love with him. It hadn't taken long for the veneer of imagined love to wear thin. Wade Barrister was a mean-spirited man, obsessed with his own importance and the idea of producing an heir to carry on the Barrister name. When ten years had passed and it became obvious that Margo was barren, he had never slept with her again.

She was sure that Wade would have demanded a divorce years ago and taken his chances for an heir with another wife, but there was a second facet to Wade's personality that was as strong as his desire to produce an heir. He was greedy. By Texas law, he would have been forced to divide all his property equally with Margo as part of the divorce settlement, and Wade would never willingly give up anything that he considered his. Especially the Circle Bar.

So instead, he'd chosen to take his pleasure with other women, all of whom Margo secretly referred to as his "whores."

And it was a particular Mexican whore who had finally produced the desired heir.

At the thought of Jesse, Margo's lips thinned again.

Their first meeting hadn't gone at all as she'd planned. She'd hoped that Jesse would be as anxious to unload the Circle Bar as she was to buy it. His hesitancy sent the first shiver of fear skating down her spine.

She dropped the curtain, blocking him from view, and whirled away from the window. Well, she assured herself, she might have lost the first battle, but she had in no way lost the war.

Jesse stood in the center of the small glen, his hands braced against his hips, his chest tight with unwanted memories. Darkness surrounded him, taunting him with shadowed ghosts he thought he had put to rest years before. He inhaled deeply, determined to keep the images at bay, and filled his senses with the bouquet of odors floating on the night air. The clean, sweet scent of freshly cut hay, the heady scent of honeysuckle that grew wild on a distant fence, the musty smell of damp leaves.

With a sigh, he lifted his face to the heavens and closed his eyes. Though he tried to keep the images from forming, they pushed at him from every side. A blanket spread on the ground, and Mandy beneath him, her body hot and damp against his. With eyes still glazed with passion, she looked up at him while a soft smile of pleasure curved the corners of her full and sensuous mouth. He could almost feel her hands on his back as she soothed his fevered flesh with soft caresses of love.

Sucking in an angry breath, he fisted his hands against his eyes. But instead of blocking the image, he only added another memory. As the vision formed, the smell of gunpowder rose, choking him, and his body recoiled with the impact of the blast that had slammed into him that night so many years ago. Instinctively, he raised a hand to his shoulder, feeling again the bullet ripping through his flesh and the fiery pain that had dragged him to the ground.

But that pain was nothing compared to the pain that tore at his heart as the memory of her voice echoed through his mind.

No, Jesse, I can't.

He lifted his fists at the dark heavens and shook them. "Damn you, Mandy!" he roared. "Damn you for choosing your father over me!"

Two

Jesse stopped his horse alongside Pete's and dug a pack of cigarettes from his shirt pocket. He shook one out, then offered the pack to Pete, the foreman of the Circle Bar.

Pete eyed him skeptically. "I prefer to roll my own," he grumbled disagreeably, but took one with a muttered, "obliged." In keeping with his own style of smoking, though, Pete pinched the filter off and tossed it to the ground.

Hiding a smile, Jesse clamped his own cigarette between his lips and dug a hand in his jeans pocket, working a lighter from its depths. He'd always had a fondness for Pete Dugan. In some ways, Pete had been more a father to him than Wade Barrister had ever been. It was Pete who'd picked Jesse up off the ground after his first bronc had thrown him, and it was Pete who had stuck Jesse's head in a horse trough when as a teenager he'd come home drunk the first time. It was also Pete who'd found Jesse the night he'd ridden his horse back into the barn after Lucas McCloud had put a bullet in his left shoulder.

Though Pete had cussed a blue streak, trying to convince Jesse he needed a doctor, he'd cleaned the wound and patched Jesse up as best as he could, then stood on the porch of the bunkhouse and watched Jesse drive away into the night.

Frowning at the unwanted memory, Jesse raked a thumb along the lighter's wheel, then cupped his hands around the flame as he drew it to the cigarette's end. Inhaling deeply, he passed the lighter to Pete, then blew out a thin stream of smoke and the memories along with it.

"Looks like you've got a good crop of calves this year," Jesse offered, gesturing to the cattle that grazed in the pasture below.

"Cain't complain."

Jesse nodded, hearing the pride behind the simple reply. "Who's giving the orders around here now that the old man's gone?"

Pete snorted. "Who do ya think?"

"And you're taking them?" Jesse asked in surprise.

"I listen, say yes'm real polite like, then do as I damn well please."

Jesse laughed, then leaned over to thump Pete on the back. "I always did like your style."

"Never did cotton to takin' orders from no woman. 'Specially one that cain't tell a bull from a steer." Pete twisted his head around just far enough to squint a look at Jesse through the smoke that curled from between his gnarled fingers. "You gonna be takin' over the reins now that you're back?"

Jesse shrugged, then squeezed the burned-out butt of his cigarette between two fingers before tossing it to the ground. "I suppose. At least until I decide what to do with the place."

"You mean you might sell?"

"I don't know," Jesse replied uncertainly. "I've got my own place up in Oklahoma now. Kind of hard to manage two places that far apart."

Pete shook his head, turning his gaze back on the cattle. "Cain't imagine the Circle Bar belongin' to anybody but a Barrister. They've owned this land long as I can remember."

They sat in silence, pondering the reality of that a moment, before Jesse said, "The old lady offered to buy me out." Though Pete's gaze never once wavered from the cattle, Jesse saw the tension mount in his shoulders on hearing of Margo's offer. "She said she'd do it to free me from any responsibilities or obligations that Wade might have burdened me with. Pretty generous of her, don't you think?"

Pete didn't answer, but continued to stare at the cattle below, his mouth set in a thin, grim line.

"Well, don't you think it's generous?" Jesse prodded.

Slowly, Pete turned his gaze on Jesse. "Margo Barrister never done nothin' in her life to benefit anybody but herself and you damn well know it, so what's your point in askin' me a damn-fool question like that?"

Jesse chuckled, then smooched to his horse, guiding him onto the narrow path that led toward the pasture below. "Just checking to make sure she hadn't softened up over the years," he called over his shoulder.

"Margo Barrister?" Pete snorted, but guided his own horse in behind Jesse's. "They'll be crankin' homemade ice cream in hell the day that old woman's heart softens.''

Pete and Jesse were headed back to the Circle Bar's headquarters when Pete suddenly pulled up and held up a hand, indicating for Jesse to stop too. ''Look over yonder,'' Pete murmured in a low voice, nodding toward the lake that lay about a quarter of a mile to the west.

Jesse looked but didn't see anything out of the ordinary. ''What?''

''Down by the water's edge under that weepin' willow.''

At that moment Jesse saw a flash of red streak from the bank and land with a silent plop, sending ripples on the water's surface radiating toward the distant shore. ''Think we caught us a trespasser?'' Jesse asked.

''Atta'd be my guess,'' Pete replied dryly.

''Well, I guess we better remind him that he's poaching on private property.''

''Damn-fool kids,'' Pete muttered irritably, leading the way. ''If I've told 'em once, I've told 'em a hunnerd times to keep off this land. And danged if I didn't just bait that hole myself last week.''

Chuckling, Jesse fell in behind him, already sympathizing with whoever was fishing Pete's favorite spot. By the time Pete got through with him, the poacher's skin would be raw from the tongue-lashing he would give him.

''Hey! You there!'' Pete yelled, reining his horse to a stop just shy of the willow tree.

A young boy, about twelve or so in Jesse's estimation, whirled, his eyes round with surprise. Immediately, he started scrambling, trying to gather up his fishing gear in order to make a run for it.

Jesse was out of the saddle and on the ground, his hand closed on the back of the boy's collar before the kid made three steps.

"Now hold on a minute," Jesse warned as the boy started twisting and fighting, trying to shake loose. When his warning wasn't heeded, Jesse grabbed the boy around the middle and hauled him hard against his side. "Now dammit, I said hold on!" Jesse yelled.

The boy immediately stilled, though Jesse could feel the tension in him beneath his arm. Not wanting to frighten the boy any more than he already was, Jesse said quietly, "Now, I'm not gonna hurt you, I just want to talk to you, all right?" When the boy slowly nodded, Jesse loosened his hold and turned him around to face him, shifting his hands to the boy's arms.

The boy jerked his head up to meet Jesse's gaze, his chin jutting in defiance. Jesse couldn't help but admire the kid's spunk. He reminded him a little of himself at that same age. But he knew he had to put the fear of God in the kid. He couldn't have him or any other trespassers thinking that the Circle Bar was open for poaching.

"Do you know that you're on private property?" Jesse asked, forcing a level of sternness into his voice.

"I didn't do nothin' wrong," the boy replied defensively. "I was just fishin', and I even threw back everything I caught."

"The point is, you're trespassing. This land belongs to the Barristers and they don't welcome uninvited guests."

The boy raised his chin a little higher, making the

cleft there a little more obvious. "The Barristers don't scare me none," he scoffed.

It was all Jesse could do not to laugh. "They don't, huh?"

"Nah. Besides, there ain't no Barristers left, 'cept the old lady and she's nothin' but an old bit—" He caught himself just shy of finishing the word, and Jesse had to wonder if he'd done so to avoid having his mouth washed out with soap in the event his mother caught wind of him cussing. "Nothin' but an old bat," the boy said instead.

Jesse had to fight hard to keep from grinning. "She is, huh?"

"Yes, sir, and that's a fact."

"Well, now, what if I was to tell you I was a Barrister?"

The boy's eyes widened before he could stop them, then narrowed to suspicious slits. "There ain't no more Barristers. Wade was the last, and he died more than a month ago."

"That's true enough...at least the part about old Wade dying." Jesse assessed the boy a moment. "If I let you go, will you promise not to run?"

The boy nodded warily, obviously still wondering about whether Jesse was in fact a Barrister.

Jesse loosened his grip on the boy's arms, then slowly dropped his hands. When the kid didn't bolt, Jesse eased a sigh of relief. "I'm Jesse Barrister, now who are you?"

"Jaime. Jaime McCloud," the boy added, squaring his shoulders proudly.

Jesse sucked in a sharp breath. *A McCloud?* Could he be Sam's or Merideth's son? Could he be... He took another hard look at the boy, taking in the cleft in the chin, the umber stain of his skin, the cowlick that kicked his hair up at the center of his forehead. No, he told himself. He couldn't be. The eyes were wrong…no—they were just right, he realized, his heart slamming hard against his chest.

They were the same unique shade of green as Mandy's.

Jesse jerked his head up to look at Pete, who remained astride his horse. But Pete's jaw was set, his eyes narrowed, and he refused to acknowledge Jesse's unasked question.

"What're you gonna do to me?" the boy asked, drawing Jesse's attention back to his face. To Jesse it was like looking in a mirror—or rather at a picture of himself at that same age.

"I—" Jesse had to clear his throat before he could answer. "I'm going to take you home to your parents."

The boy's shoulders visibly slumped.

"Do you have a problem with that?" Jesse asked.

"No, sir. It's just that I know I'm gonna get a whuppin' for sure this time," he mumbled miserably.

"And who's going to whip you?" Jesse asked, frowning, thinking that if Lucas McCloud dared to lay a hand on the kid, he'd personally make him pay.

"My mama. She's liable to skin me for sure."

"Does your mama make a habit of whipping you?"

"No, sir. But then I've never been caught on Barrister land before."

Jesse's frown deepened. It seemed that some things hadn't changed over the years. The feud between the Barristers and the McClouds still raged on.

Mandy tossed the last square of hay in the manger and closed the stall door behind her. Tucking the wire cutters into the hip pocket of her jeans, she strode angrily for the barn door. As soon as she found him, she was going to have a serious talk with her son. This was the third time this week he'd missed doing his chores.

When she stepped through the barn door, she put a hand at her brow to shade her eyes from the glaring sunlight overhead. Glancing around, she looked for a sign of Jaime. Unfortunately, the only person she saw was Gabe, her foreman, who was closing the gate on the corral behind him.

"Hey, Gabe!" she called, heading his way. "Have you seen Jaime?"

"No, ma'am. At least not lately," he added vaguely.

As she reached him, Mandy pursed her lips and folded her arms beneath her breasts. She was accustomed to her foreman and the other wranglers who worked the Double-Cross covering up her son's escapades. "Okay, so when *did* you see him last?"

Gabe dragged off his battered cowboy hat to scratch at his head. "Well, I'd guess that would've been this mornin'," he replied uneasily.

"And where was he?"

"In the barn, saddlin' his horse."

"And where was he headed?"

Gabe scratched his head again. "Cain't rightly say, though he did have his fishin' pole with him."

Mandy dropped her arms to her sides and rolled her eyes heavenward. "I swear I'm going to chain that boy to the house if he doesn't stop slipping off like this without getting his chores done first."

"Now, Miss Mandy," Gabe began.

"Don't you 'Miss Mandy' me," she scolded, shaking an accusing finger beneath his nose. "You know as well as I do that chores come first and it's high time

Jaime started acting more responsibly. He's twelve years old, after all, and you and the boys have got to quit covering for him.'' When Gabe dipped his chin, she let out a huff of breath. "Oh, for heaven's sake," she muttered. "Don't give me that hangdog look.''

Gabe lifted his head a tad, just high enough to peer at Mandy from beneath a thick overhang of bushy brows. "The boy's just got a touch of spring fever, is all. He's entitled to play hooky now and again. He's a good kid.''

If missing his chores had been the only reason for her anger, Mandy might have agreed with Gabe, because Jaime *was* a good kid. But below the anger lay a thick layer of fear. She wanted to keep her son close to home and out of harm's way until she knew for certain that Jesse Barrister had left town.

Hooking an arm through Gabe's, she headed for the barn again. "I know. It's just that—''

At that moment, Mandy heard the pounding of hoofbeats and looked back over her shoulder to see two riders loping across the pasture toward them. She immediately recognized Jaime's sorrel mare and relief weakened her knees. She shifted her gaze, squinting against the glaring sunlight in an attempt to identify the other rider.

As recognition dawned, she dug her fingers into Gabe's arm. "Oh, my God! It's Jesse!''

"Don't you worry none, Miss Mandy," Gabe hurried to assure her. "I'll handle this.''

Mandy stood at Gabe's side, watching as the riders drew near. "No," she murmured in a low voice as she withdrew her arm from his. "No," she repeated with a shake of her head. "I need to deal with this alone.''

Though she could see that Gabe wanted to argue the

point, he gave in with a sigh of defeat. "I'll be in the barn," he told her as he turned away. "If you need me, all you gotta do is give me a holler."

"Thanks, Gabe," she whispered, her gaze riveted on her son's face. She watched as he slowed his horse to first a trot, then a walk, studying his expression in an attempt to see if he showed any signs of physical or emotional damage. But all she saw was a reddening of his cheeks and downcast eyes that spoke of nothing but guilt.

But one look at Jesse's face and she knew that her secret was out. Dark accusing eyes pierced her from beneath the shadow of his black Stetson. Quickly she averted her gaze, focusing on her son again as the two riders reined their horses to a stop in front of her.

"Is there a problem?" she asked.

Jaime kept his head down, refusing to answer.

"I caught the boy trespassing on Barrister land," Jesse replied tersely.

Mandy's mouth fell open. "Jaime McCloud! What in heaven's name were you doing on the Circle Bar?"

If possible, Jaime's chin dug a deeper hole in his chest. "I didn't mean no harm," he muttered miserably. "I was just doin' a little fishin'."

"Whether you meant harm or not, you were breaking the rules. Both the Barristers' and mine." She firmed her lips to keep them from trembling, already fearing the repercussions of her son's disobedience. "Take your horse to the barn and ask Gabe to take care of him for you, then I want you to go straight to the house and wait for me there."

"Yes, ma'am," he mumbled dejectedly and turned his horse toward the barn to do her bidding.

Mandy watched Jaime ride away, feeling the heat of

Jesse's gaze on her back. Swallowing hard, she turned to face him.

Looking at him was difficult, for he hadn't changed much over the years, his handsome face the mirror image of her son's. All the old memories, the conflicting emotions he'd left her with, came rushing back and she steeled herself against their sting. "I apologize for my son's behavior and I assure you this will never happen again."

"He's mine, isn't he?"

The chilling words sent ice through Mandy's veins. Though she had feared this confrontation and had done everything in her power to avoid it, nothing had prepared her for the hate she saw in Jesse's eyes. At that moment, she knew she stood to lose Jaime, the son she had given birth to and raised on her own. But denying Jesse's accusation would do no good. "Jaime is a McCloud," she told him firmly. "I gave birth to him and I raised him alone without help from you or anybody else."

Which answered at least one of the questions that had haunted Jesse on the long ride to the Double-Cross. Mandy had never married.

"Through no fault of mine," Jesse returned. He swung down from the saddle, fisting his hand in the reins as he strode to face her, his face contorted in anger. "Why didn't you tell me I had a son?"

"Tell you!" Mandy repeated, taking a disbelieving step back. "You weren't here, remember? You took off without telling anyone where you'd gone."

Knowing she was right only made Jesse that much more angry. "I'm here now," he warned. "And I intend to claim the boy as my own."

When he whirled in the direction of the barn, Mandy

lunged, grabbing for his arm. "Jesse, wait!" He snapped his head around, his eyes burning a hole in the fingers that held his arm. Mandy quickly dropped her hand to her side. "Please," she begged him. "Don't do this."

His eyes narrowed dangerously. "Why? Are you ashamed for the boy to know that his father is half-Mexican?"

Mandy's eyes filled with frustrated tears. "No, it isn't that. It's just that he's so young, he wouldn't understand."

"What wouldn't he understand? That I'm his father or that his mother has kept that secret from him all these years?" Jesse took a threatening step closer. "Which is it, Mandy? Or has the boy never questioned his father's absence?"

Mandy closed her eyes and pressed her trembling fingers to her temples. "He's asked questions," she murmured. "I explained his Spanish heritage to him, but I told him that his father died before he was born."

"And I *would* be dead if Lucas's aim had been a little better."

Mandy paled at the memory.

"But I didn't die, Mandy," he reminded her. "I'm here and I'm going to claim my son whether you like it or not." He moved to his horse and swung up in the saddle. Folding his arms across the saddle horn, he leaned down, putting his face within a foot of Mandy's. "You've got twenty-four hours. You can pick the time and you can pick the place, but we're going to tell him. When you've made your decision, you can reach me at the bunkhouse on the Circle Bar."

Having issued the ultimatum, Jesse swung his horse around in a tight circle, dug his spurs into the gelding's sides and galloped off, leaving Mandy staring after him in a cloud of choking dust.

"Did you know he was my son?"

Pete draped his bridle over a hook and turned to Jesse on a weary sigh. "I suspected as much, though I never knowed for sure. The McClouds are pretty tight-lipped about their personal affairs."

"So no one knows?"

Pete lifted a shoulder before dragging his saddle off his horse's lathered back. "Not long after you left, Lucas shipped Mandy off to stay with some cousin of his back east. She was gone more'n a year and when she come back, she had the boy in tow. Course he was nothin' but a baby then. Rumor was she'd had an affair with some man she'd met while she was gone and he'd died before he could give the kid his name."

"And people believed the story?"

"Why not? Nobody ever knew the two of you were sneakin' around behind Lucas's back, 'cept me."

Jesse scowled at the mention of Lucas. "I didn't see him when I was over there, though I kept expecting to feel the barrel of his rifle pressed against my back."

Pete looked up in surprise. "You mean Lucas?"

"Yeah," Jesse muttered irritably. "Lucas."

"Kinda' hard to do from the grave."

Jesse jerked his head around to stare at Pete. "You mean Lucas is dead?"

"Been gone nigh on twelve years now. Had a heart attack not long after the girl brought the baby home to the Double-Cross."

Shocked by the news, Jesse could only stare. "If Lucas is gone, then who's running the place?"

"Mandy. With the help of Gabe, of course."

Jesse dropped down on a bale of hay, his legs too weak to hold him. Lucas was gone, had been for twelve years. Jesse dropped his head in his hands on a groan. If only he'd stayed, he told himself, instead of high-tailing it out of town. Without Lucas there to keep them apart, maybe he and Mandy could have been together.

No, Jesse, I can't.

Mandy's refusal seared its way through his mind and he raked his fingers through his hair as if he could tear the words from his memory. Mandy was the one who had sealed the end of their relationship, he reminded himself. Not Lucas.

He pushed himself to his feet. "I'm going to the bunkhouse," he muttered to Pete. "You coming?"

Pete stared sadly at Jesse's retreating back. "Yeah, I'll be along as soon as I finish up here."

"Maybe we should call Merideth," Sam offered quietly.

Mandy whirled from the window and the darkness beyond. "And what could Merideth possibly do?"

"Offer you a place to hide out. You should have gone to New York with her last week as she suggested, but it's not too late. You and Jaime could catch the next flight to New York and stay with her for a while. Jesse would never know to look for you there."

"That would only be delaying the inevitable."

"So you're going to tell Jaime the truth?"

Mandy lifted her hands, palms up in supplication. "What other choice do I have? You know as well as I do that Jesse has legal rights to his son. Running away isn't going to stop him from exercising those rights."

Sam blew out a long breath. "How will you explain all this to Jaime?"

Mandy turned back to the window to stare out into the darkness beyond. "I don't know," she said wearily. "I just don't know."

The phone number was easy to locate. After Sam went to bed, Mandy simply looked up the Circle Bar in the telephone directory and scanned the listings below until she found the bunkhouse. With shaking fingers, she punched in the number.

Jesse answered on the third ring.

At the sound of his sleepy voice, Mandy nearly lost her nerve. When he said "hello" a second time, she managed a faint, "Jesse?"

"Yeah?"

Nervously, she wound the phone cord around her hand. "I'd like to talk to you if I could."

"Go right ahead," came his gruff reply. "I'm listening."

Mandy wagged her head in frustration. "No, I mean in person. Could I meet you somewhere?"

There was a long stretch of silence in which Mandy held her breath.

"Where?" he finally asked.

Sagging with relief, she frantically tried to think of some place for them to meet, somewhere neutral where they wouldn't be seen or their conversation overheard. Before she could come up with a location though, Jesse offered one of his own.

"The glen. I'll meet you there at midnight."

The line went dead before Mandy could refuse.

Mandy had hoped to arrive before Jesse, needing time alone to face what had once been their secret meeting place. But he was there before her, lounging in the shadows on the trunk of a fallen oak tree, his hands stacked behind his head, his hat pulled low over his face as if he were sleeping. He'd pulled one knee up, bracing his foot against the trunk's crumbling bark. The opposite leg stretched lazily along the length of the ancient oak's trunk.

In spite of the fact that this man held her son's fate in his hands, Mandy felt her heart constrict at the sight of him. He'd been her first true love...and her last. And though she'd tried desperately over the years to do so, she'd never been able to forget him.

"Jesse?" she whispered softly, not wanting to startle him.

"Yeah?" he muttered.

Mandy twisted her hands at her waist, then, when she realized what she was doing, forced them apart. "I'm here."

Dragging a hand from beneath his head, Jesse lifted the hat from his face and turned his head to peer at her. "So I see." He rolled to a sitting position and, without ever taking his eyes off of her, snugged the hat back into position on top of his head. "Are there any guns aimed at my back?"

Her eyes widened in surprise. "Why, no! Of course not!"

"Just making sure." He hauled himself to his feet and stood, stretching. "Where's Jaime?"

"At home. In bed. I wanted to talk to you alone."

He dropped his hands to his hips. "So talk."

Mandy glanced nervously around, half expecting a ghost from the past to jump out at any moment and grab her.

"Does being here alone with me bother you?"

Mandy stiffened at the subtle taunting. "No," she

lied. "Though I wondered why you'd choose here, of all places, for us to meet."

Jesse pushed the black Stetson farther back on his head. Moonlight played over his features, revealing a sardonic smile tilting one corner of his mouth. "But this is where it all began, Mandy. This is where Jaime was conceived. To me it was the perfect place for us to discuss his future."

He nodded toward the center of the glen, and Mandy turned to look behind her. Moonlight turned the green grass growing there silver and a soft caressing breeze carried the scent of honeysuckle to her nose.

"Right there on that flat section of ground," Jesse murmured, his voice like a caress on her back. "I'd spread a blanket and wait for you while you slipped out of your father's house under the cover of darkness and sneak through the woods to meet your Mexican lover."

Tears filled Mandy's eyes and she tightened her fists at her sides to keep them at bay. *Oh, please, Jesse,* she cried silently. *Please don't do this.*

But Jesse wasn't through with her yet. Mandy had hurt him when she'd chosen her father over him and he wanted her to feel the same pain he'd felt. He wanted her to bleed in the same way he'd bled. He took a step closer, hooked a finger in the strand of hair that shadowed her face and lifted it, dropping his lips to the bare skin he exposed on her neck.

Shivers chased down Mandy's spine and she squeezed her eyes shut, willing herself not to feel anything. But heat curled in lazy spirals to settle in a pool of long-suppressed need low in her abdomen.

He lowered his hands to her shoulders and lightly squeezed, his breath hot and moist against the smooth column of her neck. "You'd burst through the shadow of the trees there, out of breath, your eyes bright with excitement, laughing as you fell into my arms. Do you remember, Mandy? Do you remember the words of love you whispered to me? Do you remember the promises you made?"

"Yes," she whispered, not wanting the reminder, not needing it. The memories had haunted her sleep for years. "Yes, I remember."

"They were lies, weren't they, Mandy?" he whispered, his fingers suddenly digging painfully into her shoulders. "All lies. Just like the lies you told my son."

Mandy whirled, wrenching free of his grasp, unable to bear hearing any more. "What do you want from me?" she cried.

"My son."

"You can't have him!"

"I don't want to take him from you, not if I can help it. I only want to share him with you and I can do that with or without your help."

The threat was there, dousing Mandy's anger with icy water, and reminding her of her need to convince him to do this her way. "I know," she said, fighting to keep the tremble from her voice. "And I've thought about what you said earlier, about you wanting to tell Jaime you're his father. You're right," she rushed on before he could interrupt her. "You deserve to share in his life."

"So what's the problem?"

Mandy dipped her chin, finding it difficult to meet his dark, penetrating gaze. "It's just that—well, it's just that I'm not sure how Jaime will accept the news." She lifted her head, begging him with her eyes to understand. "Don't you see what a shock this will be to him?"

"No more than it was to me when I discovered I had a son."

"Yes," Mandy acknowledged, only now beginning to realize what a blow that must have been for Jesse. "But Jaime knows he has a father. He also thinks he's dead. Can you imagine how difficult it will be for him when you suddenly appear and claim to be his father? Have you considered the emotional impact on a boy his age?"

"I didn't tell the boy that lie. You did."

Mandy lifted her chin defensively. "Yes, but what choice did I have when he started asking questions? You weren't here and I had no idea where you were. It was easier to tell him his father was dead than to try to explain his absence."

"So now you simply tell him the truth and admit you lied to him all those years."

Mandy narrowed an eye at him, her anger simmering back to life beneath her skin. "Oh, I see what you're trying to do. You're trying to make me the guilty party in all this while you appear free of sin and full of righteous innocence." She turned, folding her arms beneath her breasts, and strolled away a few steps, then stopped, turning to look back at him over her shoulder. "Obviously, you haven't thought all this through very well. If you had, you would see how wrong you are."

"Enlighten me," he said sarcastically.

"Jaime will want to know why you weren't there when he was born. He will resent you for not being around when he was growing up. He might even hate you. Have you considered that, Jesse?"

The fact that he hadn't was clear from his lack of response.

"I didn't think so," she replied smugly.

Jesse's mouth thinned to a grim determined line. "I'm not just going to disappear again, if that's what you're hoping. He's my son, too, Mandy. I have a right to share in his life."

"I'm not trying to deny you that," she argued fiercely. "I'm just trying to do so in such a way that Jaime isn't hurt."

"And what do you suggest we do?"

"He needs to get to know you first, develop a relationship with you. Then we'll tell him."

Jesse tossed up his hands. "And how in the hell am I supposed to develop a relationship with a boy twenty years younger than me? Besides, I'm a Barrister and he's a McCloud. It's unlikely our paths will cross."

"I've thought about that and I think I've come up with a solution."

Jesse eyed her suspiciously. "What?"

"We have a stallion that no one on the ranch can handle. I can tell Jaime that I've hired you to break him. That will gain you admittance and explain your presence on the Double-Cross while giving you an opportunity to spend time with Jaime."

Jesse looked at her incredulously. "And Jaime will believe you hired a Barrister to break a horse for you?"

Mandy lifted her chin a notch higher. "He'll believe me. The rest will be up to you."

Jesse sank down on the fallen tree trunk, dropping his face onto his hands, while Mandy waited for his answer, her breath locked tight in her lungs.

At last he lifted his head to look at her. "When do I start?"

Three

Jesse was slow to put Mandy's plan into action. Not that breaking her stallion concerned him. It was the idea of trying to win the friendship of a twelve-year-old boy that had his knees shaking…especially when he considered the fact that that twelve-year-old boy was his son. He didn't have much experience with kids and knew even less about what it took to befriend one. But he had to do it, he'd told himself repeatedly, if he wanted to claim his son.

All in all, it took him three days to get the nerve to make the drive to the Double-Cross. It was after noon on that third day when he drove his truck onto McCloud land and parked by the corral. Still a little nervous, but anxious to get things rolling, he shouldered open the door of his truck.

Before his boots even hit the ground, he found himself surrounded by the wranglers of the Double-Cross.

Their distrust was a palpable thing, their determination to protect both Mandy and the Double-Cross obvious in the hastily gathered weapons they held—a shovel, a pitchfork, a coil of rope. He thought he heard someone mutter "wetback" under his breath, but he ignored the racial slur.

Defiantly, he stood his ground.

"State your business," old Gabe demanded gruffly.

Before Jesse could answer, Mandy was pushing her way through the circle of men that surrounded him. "Hello, Jesse," she said in greeting, letting her men know by her welcome that Jesse was an invited guest on the Double-Cross. "I hope you're ready to start on that stallion."

"Yes, ma'am, I am," he returned without taking his gaze off the men, who continued to eye him suspiciously.

"Good. He's in the barn. If you'll follow me, I'll show you where you can find him."

Jesse reached inside his truck and grabbed his hat from the seat and shoved it down hard on his head. Slamming the door behind him, he stood and waited until the wranglers grudgingly shifted, creating an opening wide enough for him to pass through. But as he followed Mandy, he felt ten sets of eyes boring into his back.

Once inside the barn, he relaxed his guard, if only a little. "I gather you didn't tell your men I was coming."

Mandy stopped and turned to face him. "I wasn't sure whether or not you *would* come."

Jesse didn't like the indifference with which she regarded him. Dressed in jeans and a soft cotton shirt and with her hair pulled up in a careless ponytail, she

looked seventeen again and very much like the innocent young girl Jesse had fallen in love with. He was
tempted to reach out and yank that ribbon from her
hair, fill his hands with those long auburn tresses, and
melt that icy control with a kiss that promised to burn.

Instead, he snorted and glanced away. "As if I had
a choice." He picked up a coil of rope from the barn
floor and ran it through competent hands. "Where's
Jaime?"

"Around," she replied vaguely. "He'll show up
eventually."

"And in the meantime?"

Mandy gestured toward the far end of the long
breezeway. "You've got a horse to break."

Jesse walked with her to the remote stall where a
black stallion stood, his ears pricked forward, his dark,
dangerous eyes rolling at their approach. "What's his
name?" he asked.

"Judas."

Though he heard the level of pride in her voice, Jesse
turned to look at her in puzzlement. "Judas?" he repeated. "Kind of an odd name for a horse, isn't it?"

A smile curved at her lips as she continued to gaze
at the big black stallion. "His name suits him perfectly." She turned to Jesse, still smiling, though he
could see now that the smile came well short of reaching her eyes. "And I suggest you take heed of his
name," she warned him. "Better men than you have
learned the hard way not to turn their backs on him."

Jesse sat on the corral's top rail, a lasso hooked over
his knees, the sun warm on his back. The black stallion
paced the confines of the arena below him, blowing
and snorting and pawing at the hard-packed earth. Jesse

knew he was going to have his hands full with this one. So far, he hadn't been able to get within ten feet of him.

"Hey! What're you doin' here?"

Jesse glanced behind him to see Jaime loping across the yard toward him. Without even knowing why, he found himself grinning. "Your mama hired me to break this horse for her."

Jaime skated to a stop. "Really?" he asked in surprise, then grinned, too, proving to Jesse that Mandy was right in telling him that Jaime wouldn't question his presence on the Double-Cross. "Hey, cool!" With that Jaime clasped his hands on the fence and climbed up, planting his bottom on the rail at Jesse's side. "Have you ridden him yet?" he asked, his eyes bright with excitement.

Jesse chuckled. "No. I'm just taking his measure right now."

Jaime cocked his head, frowning. "What does that mean?"

Jesse gestured to the horse. "I'm just watching him, seeing how he responds to things. It's important to know how a horse is going to react before you climb on his back."

Jaime nodded in understanding and turned his gaze on the horse. "Gabe said he's nothin' but a widow maker and that Mama ought to shoot him before he kills somebody."

Jesse reared back, looking at Jaime askance, surprised by this bit of news. "Oh, really? And what did your mother have to say to that?"

Jaime grinned sheepishly. "I don't know. She caught me eavesdropping and clammed up before I could hear anything else."

Laughing, Jesse reached over and ruffled Jaime's hair. "It's not polite to listen in on a conversation not meant for your ears."

Jaime looked down at his boots, kicking a heel against one of the rails and dislodging a chunk of caked manure. "Yeah, that's what my mama said, too," he said ruefully.

"Your mama's right. They usually are, you know."

Jaime rolled his eyes. "They're also a pain in the butt," he muttered.

Jesse felt as if he ought to defend Mandy and mothers in general, but then thought better of it. After all, he was here to win Jaime's friendship, not build a case for Mandy. "She keeps a pretty tight rein on you, does she?" he asked instead.

Jaime huffed out a breath. "You better believe it. Especially lately."

Jesse wondered if that "especially lately" had anything to do with him. Did Mandy think he'd try to kidnap the boy or something? He shook his head. He didn't want to try to steal anything from Mandy, not even the boy's affections. He simply wanted to get to know his son and claim him as his own.

Hoping to buy some time to do just that, Jesse pulled a bandanna from his back pocket and mopped the back of his neck. "It sure is hot today."

Jaime squinted one eye up at the sun. "Yeah, it's a scorcher, all right. Wish I was down at the creek fishin' right now."

"Mmm-mmm," Jesse said with feeling. "A mess of fried catfish sure would hit the spot, wouldn't it?"

Jaime glanced up at him in surprise. "You like to fish?"

"Sure do. You're not the only boy to poach in his

neighbor's pond. When I was about your age I used to sneak over to the Double-Cross and fish that old pond that lies in that strip of bottom land. You know where I'm talking about?''

''Yeah! There's a couple of felled trees that the cat-fish like to swim up under and nap. You wanna go fishin'?'' he asked, nearly falling off the fence in his rush to issue the invitation.

Although that was exactly what Jesse had been hinting at, he replied uncertainly, ''Well, I don't know. What do you suppose your mother would have to say about you scooting off in the middle of the day?''

''I bet she wouldn't mind if you were going along!'' Jaime was already clambering down. ''Let's go ask her.''

Trying to hide his pleasure at the thought of spending an afternoon with his son, Jesse jumped down and followed Jaime to the house. But at the back door, he hesitated, unsure whether Mandy's invitation to the Double-Cross included entry into her private quarters.

''Come on!'' Jaime encouraged him. ''Mama's probably in her office workin'.''

Dragging off his hat, Jesse stepped inside, closing the door softly behind him, and followed Jaime through the kitchen and down a long hall. At the door to the office he stopped, the hairs on his neck prickling.

Jaime might have called this his mama's office, but evidence of Lucas McCloud's prior claim to the space was apparent everywhere Jesse looked. The walls were covered with trophies from Lucas's hunting and fishing expeditions—a twelve-point rack of antlers, an elk's head, a swordfish posed as if it had just burst through the water's surface. A locked case held a small arsenal of guns. On the floor in front of a massive desk lay a thick bearskin rug. Behind the masculine desk sat Mandy, her chin tipped up from her work, her green eyes filled with what Jesse could only define as distrust.

Feeling compelled to defend his presence, Jesse explained, "Jaime invited me to go fishing, but I told him we'd need to ask you first."

Slowly Mandy rose from the deep leather chair, clutching the pen she'd been using as if it were a weapon she might need to defend herself. "I see." She forced her gaze to her son's. "Have you finished your chores?"

"Yes, ma'am," he said proudly.

"What about emptying the trash in the kitchen?"

Jaime's expression fell. "No, I forgot about that one."

"You'll have to finish *all* your chores before you can play."

Jaime hung his head and gave the bearskin rug a stab with a frustrated toe. "Ah, Mom," he complained dejectedly. "Can't it wait 'til later?"

"You know the rules," she reminded him firmly.

Jaime lifted his gaze to Jesse's, obviously knowing it was fruitless to argue with his mother. "Wait for me, okay? It won't take me a minute, I swear." With that he was gone, leaving Jesse standing before the desk, his hat in his hand.

"Does that go for me, too?"

Mandy shifted her gaze from the doorway her son had just disappeared through to look at Jesse. "What?" she asked in confusion.

"Do I have to finish my chores, too?"

Mandy frowned, then sank back onto her chair and turned her attention back to her work. "My rules only apply to my son."

Jesse took a step closer, peering at the ledger book that was spread on the desk. "From what I hear, they apply to the men who work the Double-Cross, as well."

Without looking up, Mandy shifted the pen back into position between her fingers and began making notations on the page. "Yes, though I suspect there are a few who resent taking orders from a woman."

That his presence made her nervous was obvious and only served to goad Jesse into wanting to rattle her a little bit more. He levered a hip on the corner of the desk and hooked his hat on his knee. "What are you working on?"

"Not that it's any of your business," she replied, trying her best to ignore him, "but I'm recording the births of all the new foals."

Grinning, Jesse leaned closer and almost laughed when he saw her fingers convulse on the pen. "Looks like your mares have dropped quite a few foals this year," he commented lazily. "You must have one hell of a good stud."

He watched the heat crawl up her neck at the inflection he'd purposefully put on the words "you" and "stud."

"We use two," she replied through tight lips.

"Is Judas one of them?"

"Yes. He has excellent bloodlines. Satan sired him."

Jesse remembered Satan well—the black stallion that only Lucas McCloud had ridden. "Jaime tells me that Judas is a widow-maker. Is that why you hired me on to break him? Are you hoping that he'll kill me and I won't be around to claim my son?"

Incensed, Mandy jumped to her feet, tossing her pen to the desk. "Certainly not! I would never hire someone to break a horse if I didn't think he was more than capable of handling the task.''

Jesse stood, too, and shifted until he was between her and the desk. "So you think I'm capable, do you?" He touched a finger to the hollow of her throat where her pulse throbbed. When she stiffened, he smiled in satisfaction. She might pretend indifference to him, but he knew better.

Angrily, Mandy batted his hand away. "If I didn't think you could handle Judas, I'd never have suggested that you try to break him."

With a studied slowness, Jesse let his gaze slide up the smooth column of her throat, over the flush on her cheeks, until his eyes met hers. Beneath the fear, he was surprised to see that desire had darkened their green depths…and knew at that moment how best to punish her for what she'd done to him.

"That's nice to know," he said slowly. He took a step closer, until his body brushed hers. "But I'm capable of taming more than just a wild horse," he murmured suggestively. "I can—"

"I'm ready!"

The announcement came from the hallway, allowing Jesse just enough time to step away from Mandy and pretend to admire a plaque on the wall before Jaime burst through the open doorway. Turning, he smiled at the boy. "Me, too, son."

He slung an arm around Jaime's shoulders and shot Mandy a wink that had her cheeks turning a brighter red. "I'll see you later."

With her heart in her throat, Mandy watched them file out of her office, laughing and talking like two old friends. Weak-kneed, she sank to the leather chair. Grabbing the desk's edge, she drew the chair back into place, then propped her elbows on the ledger and flattened her palms against her burning cheeks. How can he do this to me? she cried silently. Better yet, *why* is he doing this to me?

He was purposefully baiting her, she was sure, trying to incite some kind of response from her. He had acted similarly at the glen when they had met several days before. But why? He'd certainly made his feelings for her clear enough. He hated her...or at the very least he resented her for keeping Jaime a secret from him.

The fact that she'd responded each time to his touch both angered and shamed her. She lifted her head from her hands and pressed trembling fingers to her lips as she stared at the empty doorway.

Oh, God, how she'd missed his touch.

Mandy heard Jaime and Jesse's arrival before she actually saw them. They returned to the house in much the same manner as they'd left several hours before: laughing and talking like two old friends. She knew she should be grateful for the ease with which her son accepted Jesse's offer of friendship—after all, that was the purpose behind Jesse's presence on the Double-Cross. But she couldn't help but resent it, as well. For twelve years she had been Jaime's only parent, the most important adult in his life...and now Jesse threatened that relationship.

Forcing back the jealousy, she opened the back door and stepped out onto the patio. "Well!" she exclaimed, offering them both a smile. "The mighty fishermen return. Did y'all catch anything?"

Grinning, Jaime held up a stringer of catfish for her inspection.

"My, my, my," she murmured in approval. "That looks like enough for dinner."

"That's what me and my *amigo* were thinkin', too," Jaime told her as he handed over the stringer.

Mandy's eyebrows shot up. *"Amigo?"* she repeated.

Jaime grinned. "It's Spanish for friend. Jesse taught me some Spanish words while we were fishin'."

"Oh," Mandy murmured, cutting a glance at Jesse. His eyes seemed to dare her to find fault with him.

"Jesse's gonna eat with us, okay?"

Mandy snapped her gaze back to her son. Though she would have loved to have said no, she couldn't ignore the hope in her son's eyes...or the challenge in Jesse's. Smiling sweetly, she passed Jesse the stringer. "Sure. Why not? He can clean the fish while you go and take a shower."

"A shower? But—"

"No buts, young man. You smell like you've rolled in fish bait."

Obviously knowing by the unrelenting look in his mother's eyes that the shower battle was one he was sure to lose, Jaime scuffed into the house, wearing a king-size pout and leaving Mandy and Jesse alone.

Anxious to escape Jesse's nearness, Mandy nodded toward a stainless-steel table that sat on the edge of the patio. "You can clean the fish there. Knives and bowls are stored underneath and you can use the hose hooked up by the kitchen window for water." She started to turn away, but Jesse's voice stopped her.

"Thank you."

Though she might have pretended to think that he was thanking her for letting him know where everything was, Mandy knew by the level of emotion in his voice and the gratitude in his dark eyes that he was thanking her for a whole lot more. He was thanking her for allowing him to spend more time with Jaime.

"I'm only doing what's fair," she murmured, then turned and headed for the kitchen door before he could say more.

From the kitchen window Mandy had a perfect view of Jesse cleaning the fish. Not that she was watching him, she assured herself. He just happened to be in her line of vision each time she glanced up from the potatoes she was peeling.

He'd taken off his shirt—in deference to the heat, she supposed—and with every slice of the knife he held, muscles bunched and rolled on his back while sweat ran down his spine in narrow rivulets to dampen the waist of his jeans. His shoulders were as wide as she remembered them, tapering down to a narrow waist and hips. He stood with one leg cocked, throwing one hip a little higher than the other, and Mandy couldn't prevent her gaze from sliding lower, over the swell of buttocks beneath the worn denim, to muscled thighs and calves and finally to boots scarred from years of use.

Resting her wrists on the edge of the sink, Mandy let the paring knife go limp in her hand. His body had once been as familiar to her as her own, she remembered sadly. She'd known every scar and its cause, every sensitive spot and whether it would elicit a chuckle or a moan of pleasure at her touch. She'd touched even the most intimate parts of him and done so without fear or shame. She'd loved him and he'd loved her, just as thoroughly, just as completely.

While she watched, her thoughts rooted in the past, Jesse set the bowl of filleted catfish aside and picked up the hose again. Dipping his head, he placed the spout on his hair, letting the water run down his back and over his chest. Shifting the hose to a position between his pressed knees, he filled his cupped hands with water and splashed his face, scrubbing his hands up and down its length and across the back of his neck.

Without thinking, Mandy laid the paring knife aside, went to the pantry for a towel, and stepped outside.

"I thought you might need this."

Jesse glanced up, blinking water from his eyes, to find Mandy standing in front of him, offering him a towel. The desire was there in her eyes again, he noted, minus the layer of fear that had covered it before.

Warily, he accepted the towel. "Thanks," he mumbled as he dragged it down his face, obscuring his view of her. When he dropped the towel, he saw that her gaze had lowered and was fixed on his chest. She reached out and placed a trembling finger against the scar her father's bullet had left on his shoulder. When she lifted her face to his again, he saw that her eyes were filled with tears.

"I'm so sorry," she whispered huskily.

Something in her eyes had Jesse reaching up and catching her hand in his before he even realized what he was doing. He pressed her fingertips against the scar, absorbing the warmth of her skin into his. "You didn't pull the trigger," he reminded her. "Lucas did."

"Yes, but—"

He stepped closer, placing a finger against her lips. "I never blamed you for Lucas shooting me."

In dark eyes that seemed to pull her closer, Mandy searched for some sign that he'd forgiven her for the other blow, the one to his heart. "But you've never forgiven me, have you? For refusing to—"

"Hey! Where is everybody?"

Jesse dropped Mandy's hand at the sound of Jaime's voice and picked up the bowl of catfish fillets. "Out here!" he called back. "Are you hungry?"

The screen door slapped open and Jaime charged through it, his wet hair gleaming as raven-black as Jesse's in the fading sunlight. "You bet! Is everything ready?"

Jesse sat with his shoulders pressed against the wall of the bunkhouse and his boots propped on the low railing that bordered the structure's narrow front porch. Darkness stretched in front of him while a herd of mosquitoes buzzed at his ear. Irritably he swatted at them while he silently cursed himself for a fool.

He should have just knocked her hand away when Mandy had dared to touch him, he told himself. But, oh no, not Jesse! Fool that he was, he'd let himself be suckered by a set of tear-filled eyes.

He knew damn good and well that if Jaime hadn't shown up when he had, he'd have had Mandy in his arms again, kissing away the telltale tears and filling his hands with those delicious curves.

And Jesse didn't need or want the distraction. He'd learned long ago not to trust Mandy. She made promises she didn't intend to keep and Jesse wasn't about to fall prey to her lies anymore. He'd done so once and had spent years trying to forget.

He had a son now. And his son was all he wanted from Mandy McCloud.

Margo stepped inside the barn, squinting to adjust to the sudden change in light. About halfway down the alley, Pete stood, saddling his horse.

"Where is he?" she snapped impatiently.

Pete turned his head, sparing her a look. "If you're referrin' to Jesse, he ain't here."

"I can see that. Where is he?"

Pete turned back to his horse, hooking a stirrup over the saddle horn. "Where he goes and what he does is his business, not mine."

Margo folded her arms beneath her breasts, glaring at Pete's back. "I should've known I couldn't depend on you to offer any information as to his whereabouts."

"Then why'd you ask?" Pete muttered dryly.

Incensed by his blatant disregard of her position as mistress of the Circle Bar, Margo sucked in an angry breath. The man would never have dared to talk to her in such a high-handed way when Wade was alive. But obviously, with Jesse's arrival to claim his inheritance, Pete no longer felt he had to show Margo the respect she was due. "You always did try to protect him," she said bitterly. "Even when he was a child."

"Somebody had to look after the boy," Pete replied. "Neither you nor Wade seemed to want the job."

"It wasn't my place to look after him! He was Wade's bastard, not mine."

At the word 'bastard,' Pete slowly turned. "Better watch your mouth, Margo," he warned dangerously. "That 'bastard' you're referrin' to is the head of this outfit now."

Piercing him with a damning look, Margo whirled away. "Not if I have any say in the matter," she muttered under her breath.

And as to learning where Jesse spent his time when away from the Circle Bar…well, she had other sources to turn to.

* * *

Jesse stood in the center of the Double-Cross's corral, his gaze fixed on the prancing stallion. He'd worked with the horse for four days and he was no closer to putting a saddle on him than he was on the first day he'd arrived. Sweat soaked his back and stung his eyes. "Ho, boy," he murmured in a soothing voice. "Ho, now."

In answer, the stallion tossed his head and reared, clawing at the air.

"Yeah, you're the king of the jungle, all right. Nobody's denying you that." Jesse took a step closer, keeping his hand extended. "But even the king of the jungle can be tamed," he muttered under his breath. "And, buddy, I'm the lion tamer, so you might as well lie down and admit defeat so we can both get out of this heat."

The stallion seemed to think that was funny because he lifted his head and let out a loud, piercing whinny that seemed to negate Jesse's boast before he dropped his head and charged straight at him.

Jesse made the fence in the nick of time, sticking a boot between the iron rails halfway up and projecting himself over the top one to land with a muffled "Umph!" on the other side.

"Nice landing."

Jesse opened one eye to see Gabe standing over him. With a groan, he closed it again and struggled to ascertain—without moving—if he'd broken anything.

"You okay?" Gabe asked, this time with a touch of concern in his voice.

"Yeah, I think so." Jesse pushed himself to his elbows and eyed the black devil on the other side of the fence. "No thanks to our friend Judas."

"He's a mean one, all right," Gabe agreed with a

brisk jerk of his chin. "I told Mandy she oughta jist forget about breakin' him and turn him out with the mares and let him do what he was born to do, but she's bound and determined to make a saddle horse out of him yet."

Jesse sat up a little straighter. "You mean to tell me that Mandy's planning on riding this horse?"

Gabe shook his head as if he couldn't believe it either. "That's what she says."

Jesse pushed himself to his feet. He scraped his hat off the ground, gave it a good whack against the side of his leg, then rammed it on his head. "Well, we'll just see about that," he muttered angrily.

When he reached the back door he didn't bother to knock, but charged right into the kitchen and down the hall, leaving a trail of dust behind him and the angry echo of a slammed door. He didn't stop until he stood in front of her desk. Planting his hands on the oak surface, he pushed his face to within an inch of hers. "Why in the hell didn't you tell me that you planned on riding that black devil?"

Mandy reared back, putting as much distance between them as possible. "I suppose you're referring to Judas."

"And who the hell else do you think I'd be referring to? Damn it, Mandy!" he roared. "You don't have any business on that horse's back. He's crazy, a killer, and even if I succeed in breaking him to a saddle, I'll never be able to break his spirit, and you damn well know it."

"I didn't ask you to break his spirit," she replied, pushing to her feet. "I wouldn't want you to, even if you could."

Jesse rounded the desk. "So you admit that he's a

killer,'' he said, pointing an accusing finger beneath her nose.

Mandy pushed his hand away. "I didn't admit to any such thing. I merely agreed that Judas is high-spirited."

"A killer," Jesse insisted. "And I'll be damned if I'll stand by and watch you crawl on his back."

"And what gives you the right to tell me what I can and can not do?"

"You're the mother of my son, that's what gives me the right. Jaime needs you. He needs his mother and you have no right to jeopardize your life and Jaime's happiness just to prove something to Lucas McCloud."

Mandy's head snapped up at the mention of her father, the gold in her green eyes striking fire. "Lucas has nothing to do with this."

"Oh, doesn't he?" Jesse mocked. "Aren't you trying to prove to your father's ghost and everyone who works for you that you are as strong, as stubborn as Lucas was by riding the son of the horse that he broke and rode himself?"

Mandy felt heat burn her cheeks as the truth behind Jesse's accusation hit a little too close to home. "That's ridiculous," she muttered as she brushed past him.

Jesse caught her arm and swung her back around to face him. "Is it?"

Mandy didn't attempt to break free but forced herself to maintain an air of coolness when she replied. "Careful, Jesse. You might make me think you really care what happens to me."

All the anger, all the frustration suppressed for years had Jesse hauling her up against his chest. The slam of her body against his dislodged his hat and it fell to the hardwood floor and bounced against his leg, but Jesse merely kicked it aside.

The fear in her eyes, the stiffness of her body only served to incense him more. With a feral growl, he crushed his mouth over hers, punishing her with his lips while he banded his arms around her, holding her in place. He felt the claw of her fingernails on his back, but he ignored her struggles for freedom, determined to make her pay for every sin she'd ever committed against him, both known and unknown.

Within seconds he realized his mistake. Instead of savoring the revenge he so justly deserved, he found himself focusing instead on the press of her breasts against his chest, the fullness of the lips beneath his, the taste that he thought he'd forgotten.

Slowly he softened the kiss, sweeping his tongue across the bow of her lips, teasing the corners of her mouth, until at last she surrendered, parting her lips for him on a soft moan. He pressed her closer still, probing the velvet softness of her mouth. He found her tongue and mated it with his, drawing hers with an aching slowness into his mouth.

Mandy was sure she would die from the heat that ravaged her body. She didn't want this, she told herself even as she lifted her hands, threaded her fingers through his hair and drew his face closer. She didn't want to feel this aching need for Jesse again. But it was there, curling like a fist low in her belly and spreading like molten honey to her limbs, making her weak and helpless in his arms.

As if he sensed her need, he slipped his hands from her back to curve over her buttocks and draw her hard against his groin. A moan started low in his throat and rose to vibrate against her lips.

Jesse. Oh, Jesse, she silently cried. *I've missed this, you, so much.*

Wanting to share with him her feelings if only by touch, she dragged her hands to his face, molding the sharp planes of his cheekbones, tracing the strong line of his jaw and pressing her thumb to the cleft in his chin. With a sigh drawn from the familiarity of each of those features, she let her hands drop to his chest. Heat, comfort, strength. She found each in the padded muscles beneath her palms, in the pounding of his heart, which echoed that of her own.

But then, as suddenly as he'd taken her, he was gone, and her palms rested against nothing but air. Her breathing ragged, Mandy opened her eyes to find him standing with his back to her. His head was dipped low on his chest, his hands were braced at his hips while he pulled in a long, shuddering breath.

Feeling the sting of his rejection, she whispered brokenly, "Don't ever do that again."

Jesse bent to scoop his hat from the floor without looking at her. "Don't worry," he said as he strode for the office door. "I don't plan to."

Four

"Hey! Watch out!"

Before the warning even registered through the fog of anger blinding him, Jesse had plowed into the woman who'd shouted it. With a grunt of surprise as their bodies connected, he instinctively grabbed for her, catching her at the waist and twisting his body to take the brunt of the fall as they both toppled to the ground. A split second after his back hit the hard-packed dirt, a black bag slammed into the side of his head.

"Get your hands off me!"

Jesse immediately dropped his hands from the woman's waist and managed to focus on two spots of brown among the stars that danced before his eyes.

"Sam?" he asked uncertainly as he gazed up into the face of Mandy's younger sister.

The woman in question shoved hard against his chest, already pushing to her feet, her cheeks a flaming red. "Well, at least you're not totally blind," she muttered while she dusted indignantly at the legs of her jeans. "You at least recognized me."

Jesse pushed himself to his elbows and winced, drawing himself to a sitting position to inspect a burning elbow. "Sorry," he muttered as he dabbed at a spot of blood already staining his shirt's blue fabric. "I wasn't paying attention to where I was going."

"You're telling me?" With a huff of impatience, Sam stooped to reclaim her bag. "I would've guessed that right off." As she straightened, she caught a glimpse of Jesse's sluggish movements. "Are you hurt?" she asked, narrowing a wary eye at him.

"Just a little scratch," he answered though he kept the arm tucked to his middle as he used his other hand to push himself to a standing position.

Sam shifted the bag and reached for his wrist. Angling his arm for a better look, she plucked a corner of the torn fabric and frowned at the cut beneath. "Come on inside the barn and I'll clean it up for you."

The offer was sincere enough, even if it was grudgingly offered, but Jesse was anxious to get off the Double-Cross and put as much distance as possible between himself and Mandy. "That's not necessary. I can—"

"Oh, don't be such a baby," she snapped impatiently and spun away, leaving him no choice but to follow.

Once inside the lab room where all the ranch's veterinary supplies were stored, Sam tossed her bag on the counter and rolled up her sleeves. "You might want to slip that arm out of your sleeve," she suggested without meeting his gaze.

While Jesse shucked off his shirt, Sam opened the bag. After twisting on the tap at the sink, she motioned

Jesse to join her. "Stick your arm under here and let's get you cleaned up so I can get a better look."

Reluctantly, Jesse obeyed and Sam gently dabbed at the wound. "Not too deep," she muttered to herself as she prodded the torn flesh. "A little antibiotic ointment and a butterfly bandage ought to do."

"Is that a medical opinion, or just a guess?"

"A medical opinion. I'm a vet," she added for clarification as she laid out the items she'd need. "And in case you're worried, humans aren't all that different from animals in a lot of respects."

Resigned to the fact that he wouldn't be leaving the Double-Cross for a few minutes more, Jesse leaned back against the counter. "A vet, huh?" The choice of career seemed perfect for the tomboy Jesse remembered. He turned his arm, offering her easier access as she moved in front of him.

"Yeah. It suits me." She squirted a generous supply of ointment on her finger, then hesitated, as if unable or unwilling to touch him.

"I won't bite," he couldn't help teasing.

Sam snapped her gaze up to meet his, a frown gathering between her brows. But she obviously decided not to rise to the bait, choosing instead to ask a question of her own. "What were you in a such an all-fired hurry for, anyway?"

Jesse frowned too at the reminder of the intimacy he'd just shared with Mandy. "Just anxious to get home," he replied vaguely.

Sam paused in her ministrations to glance up at him. Just as quickly, she averted her gaze. "Seen Jaime around?"

"No. He's spending the day with some friend of his."

Sam nodded knowingly. "That would be Davie. The two are joined at the hip. They usually spend every Friday together."

That Sam was more familiar with his son's activities than he was, hurt Jesse in a way he hadn't expected. "I suppose you know the boy fairly well?"

Sam glanced up again, but this time held his gaze. "If you're asking me if I know he's your son, yes, I do, and I also know why you're here."

"And how do you feel about that? About me wanting to claim my son?"

Sam dropped her gaze, turning her attention back to her work. She plucked a bandage from her bag, and peeled off the protective covering. "What I feel isn't important."

"But you *do* have an opinion," Jesse insisted.

Sam drew the two sections of skin together and pressed the bandage into place, her touch gentle in spite of the frown that still creased her forehead. When she finished, she stepped back quickly, wiping her hands on the seat of her jeans as if touching him repelled her. "I won't see either one of them hurt," she warned and turned away. "Not Jaime and not Mandy."

"And you think that is my intention? To hurt them?"

"Sometimes we hurt people whether we intend to or not," she replied.

Jesse couldn't help wondering if she was speaking from personal experience. Mandy wasn't the only one of his daughters that Lucas had chosen to bully. Mandy had shared with Jesse stories of her father's dominance over her sisters, as well as herself. But something in Sam's voice made him wonder if maybe she was referring to someone other than Lucas. He shook off the distracting thought. Sam was entitled to her secrets. "Did Lucas make it hard on Mandy when he found out she was pregnant?"

Though Jesse could see the tension tighten on Sam's back, she merely lifted a shoulder in a shrug as she methodically placed her supplies back into the bag. "Let's just say that the idea of having a grandson with Barrister blood running in his veins didn't exactly please him."

"Did the boy suffer as a result?"

"No," she replied without hesitation. "Jaime was just a baby when Daddy died and too young to be affected by Lucas's resentment of him."

"What about Mandy?"

Sam looked up at him, her eyes guarded, protecting any secrets that might be hidden behind them. "You'll have to ask Mandy that question. It isn't my place to say."

You'll have to ask Mandy that question. It isn't my place to say.

Throughout the drive back to the Circle Bar, Jesse wondered at Sam's odd comment. Obviously, Lucas McCloud had been hard on Mandy, or Sam would have denied his question outright. And though he kept telling himself it shouldn't matter to him one way or the other, he couldn't ease the itch of guilt that sprang to life between his shoulder blades for the part he'd played in Mandy's suffering.

And that guilt only reminded him of his last encounter with Mandy less than an hour before.

He drew a shaking hand across his mouth, remembering the taste of her, mindful of the memories that kiss had awakened, of how far he would've liked to take that kiss. As the last thought rose, he pressed the accelerator a little closer to the floor, anxious to escape the temptation.

Trouble, he warned himself, scowling at the road ahead. That's what Mandy meant for him. Nothing but trouble. Not only had she chosen her father over him, but she'd kept his son a secret from him...and Jesse would never forgive her for that.

But if he thought he'd outrun all his problems by simply leaving the Double-Cross, Jesse was badly mistaken. As he pulled his truck up by the barn on the Circle Bar, he saw Margo and Pete standing almost nose-to-nose in the barn's shadow. From the defensive stance each had assumed, Jesse figured that they weren't discussing anything as innocuous as the weather.

On a sigh, he shoved open the door of his truck and the piercing shrill of Margo's voice hit him with full force.

"Is there a problem here?" he asked, knowing it was up to him to act as referee if one was needed.

Margo whirled, her eyes blazing. "I want this man fired immediately!"

Jesse gave Pete a cursory glance, noting the flush of anger on the old man's face, before turning his gaze fully on Margo. "And may I ask why?"

"He refuses to follow my orders! I told him two weeks ago to sell those cows in the west pasture and have only just discovered that he blatantly ignored my instructions. He's nothing but a stubborn old fool who insists on doing things his way."

Jesse turned to look at Pete. "What do you have to say about all this?"

The hiss of breath behind Jesse told him that he had

insulted Margo by asking for Pete's take on the situation instead of firing him on the spot.

Pete shot Margo one last thunderous look before turning his attention to Jesse. "She's talkin' about those heifers I showed you last week when we was out ridin'. Wade and me handpicked those heifers to replenish the herd and I'm not about to sell 'em when we need 'em for breedin' purposes. I'd jist have to go out and buy some new ones to replace 'em and that's jist plain foolishness, if you ask me."

"And who asked you?" Margo interjected, her voice rising as quickly as the color on her face.

"I did," Jesse replied, turning to face her. "And since I'm the one in charge here, Margo, not you, I have to agree with Pete's decision. The heifers stay."

The blood from Margo's face slowly drained away, leaving her cheeks pale, her lips trembling with silent rage at what Jesse was sure she considered his traitorous decision. Without another word to either of the men, she whirled and stalked back to the house.

Jesse and Pete stood side by side and watched her go.

"I'm sorry you got dragged in on this one," Pete mumbled in apology. "She'll make you pay for takin' my side for sure."

Jesse turned to look at Pete in puzzlement. "How so?"

Pete dragged off his hat and mopped his brow with his shirtsleeve. "I don't know. But she'll figger out a way. She always does."

Jesse clamped a hand on his old friend's shoulder. "Don't you worry your old bald head about Margo," he teased, trying to make light of what he was sure was an accurate assumption on Pete's part. "I can handle any trouble she tries to throw my way."

Pete glanced up, the look in his eyes as bleak as the clouds that were beginning to gather overhead. He settled his hat back on his head with a sigh. "I hope so, son. I sure hope so."

Jesse considered avoiding the Double-Cross altogether and focusing instead on the problems building on the Circle Bar, but by Monday morning the thought of Jaime and the progress he'd made in developing a relationship with his son had him shoving the tempting thought aside. The Circle Bar meant nothing to him, but his son, he was slowly beginning to realize, meant everything.

When he arrived at the Double-Cross, he found Jaime sitting on the corral fence, waiting for him. The fact that he was pleased Jesse enormously.

"Hey, Jesse!" Jaime called as he jumped down from the fence and loped toward him.

"Hey, yourself," Jesse replied as he leaned over to draw a coiled rope from the bed of his truck. "What are you up to?" he asked as he hooked the lasso over his shoulder.

"Oh, 'bout five-one," Jaime shot back, grinning.

Jesse grabbed him in a headlock and rubbed his knuckles over the boy's hair. "You've got a smart mouth on you, you know it?"

Laughing, Jaime wrestled free. "That's what they tell me." He stepped back, dragging a hand over his mussed hair, but that cowlick shot right back up like a rooster's tail in the center of his forehead. "The truth is, I was waiting for you."

Jesse felt a bubble of pride swell in his chest. "Is that a fact?"

"Yep. Mama said for me to tell you that you won't be able to work with Judas today."

The bubble deflated just a little. "Oh? And why not?"

"He's out on stud. Mr. Phillips from over in San Antonio picked him up yesterday. He'll probably have him back in a couple of days, though."

Jesse frowned at the news. Why hadn't Mandy called him and saved him the trip over? he wondered, then quickly dismissed the thought, realizing that she probably wasn't any more anxious to talk to him than he was to talk to her. Not after what had happened between them.

Sliding the rope from his shoulder, he smoothed his fingers over the rough hemp, his frown deepening as he realized that without Judas there to work with, he didn't have any excuse to stay on at the Double-Cross with his son.

"Are you any good with that?" Jaime asked, nodding toward the lasso Jesse held.

"Good enough. Why?"

"With Judas gone and all, I was wonderin'...." Jaime ducked his head and dug the toe of his boot into the ground.

"Wondering what?" Jesse prodded.

"Well, I was wonderin' if maybe you'd have the time to teach me how to throw a rope."

If the situation had been a life-and-death one and Jaime had asked Jesse to donate a kidney to him, Jesse would have been just as willing. His love for the boy had grown that strong. "I think I could handle that." He slung an arm around Jaime's shoulders and turned him toward the barn. "Think we can scare up a bale of hay to practice on?"

Jaime grinned up at him, almost dancing at Jesse's side. "You bet!"

Together the two hauled a bale from the barn and out into the yard. Jesse took a plastic steer's head from the toolbox in his truck and wired it into place on one end of the bale. Shaking out the lasso, he positioned his hands, demonstrating for Jaime. "Keep a loose grip, but firm enough to maintain control." He held the rope out to Jaime, then adjusted the boy's fingers. "The throw's all in the wrist," he instructed, keeping his hands over his son's. "Soft roll to the right, bringing the lasso up and over your head." He went through the motions with him, then stepped back, giving Jaime a chance to get the feel of the rope.

When Jaime brought the rope up over his head and immediately smacked himself in the forehead with it, Jesse bit back a smile. "A little higher," he offered, "and sweep it out a little more in front of you before drawing it up."

With his lower lip caught between his teeth, Jaime gave it another try, this time missing his head before letting the lasso drop. He turned, grinning. "Like that?"

Jesse laughed and clapped him on the back. "Just like that. Ready to see if you can lasso that steer?" he asked, gesturing toward the bale of hay he'd set out.

Jaime let out a nervous breath. "Yeah. I guess." He shifted the rope in his hands, then drew it up and over his head as Jesse had instructed, gave it a few twirls, then let it fly. The lasso sailed through the air, hitting the ground a good five feet from the bale of hay. The end of the rope hit about six feet behind it.

Jesse tossed back his head and laughed. "I guess I forgot to mention that you're supposed to hold on to the end of the rope."

Jaime turned, grinning sheepishly. "Yeah, I guess you did."

Together they walked to the bale and Jesse stooped to retrieve the rope, skilfully drawing it back into a loose coil. Taking the lasso, he shook it out, curled it back into position, then offered it to Jaime. "How about another try?"

"Yeah, sure."

Jesse stepped back while Jaime positioned himself for the throw.

"You got any kids?"

The question came out of nowhere and nearly knocked Jesse on his butt. Unconsciously, he reached for the pack of cigarettes he kept in his shirt pocket and shook one out, his fingers trembling. "Why do you ask?" he asked as he clamped the cigarette between his teeth and dug in his jeans pocket for his lighter.

"Just wondered." Jaime turned at the grate of the lighter's wheel, his eyes zeroing in on the cigarette. He grinned. "Mama says those things'll stunt your growth."

Realizing what he'd done, Jesse jerked the cigarette from his mouth and dropped it, then crushed it beneath the heel of his boot. "She's right," he mumbled, only just becoming aware of his responsibility in setting a good example for his son. "Bad habit."

Jaime turned back, drawing a bead on the steer's head. "Yeah, she says that, too." He lifted the rope and made a slow circle over his head. "Course she says that about everythin' that's any fun." He let the lasso fly and it smacked the steer's head before falling to the ground. His shoulders sank in frustration.

Thankful that, for the moment at least, Jaime had forgotten his original question, Jesse called out to him, "Well, at least you're getting closer."

Mandy glanced out the window of her office again and groaned. Was he never going to leave? she wondered in growing frustration. A quick look at her wristwatch and she knew she couldn't put off going outside any longer.

In a last-ditch effort to avoid having to meet Jesse face-to-face, she paused on the back door step and yelled, "Jaime!"

She listened for his answering call and frowned at her own cowardice. Knowing darn well that her voice wouldn't carry all the way to the barn, she was left with no choice but to go and collect her son personally.

Squaring her shoulders, she strode in the direction of the barnyard where she'd caught glimpses all afternoon of her son and Jesse throwing a rope around. She knew she should applaud Jesse's patient efforts in coaching Jaime, but darn it, she couldn't! She'd hoped that with Judas gone she'd get a few more days' reprieve before she had to face Jesse again. Their last encounter had left her feeling bruised and battered and way too vulnerable.

"Jaime!" she called again when she drew near enough to be heard.

He turned his head and looked in her direction. "Over here, Mama! Come and watch me rope this steer."

Though Mandy would have preferred her son to come to her, she knew she couldn't deny him the pleasure of showing off his newly learned skill. With a sigh, she picked up the hem of her long broomstick skirt and continued on.

"Watch this, Mama." Turning back to his target, Jaime lifted the rope and twirled it over his head a couple of times and let it go. Mandy watched the lasso float through the air and land around the steer's head, barely clearing its fake horns. Jaime gave the rope a hard tug, setting it in place.

"That's great, son," she said, clapping her hands to show her approval. "But it's time to come in now."

"But, Mama—" he began.

"No buts, Jaime. I'm going out tonight and Sam promised to keep you. Unfortunately, she's stuck out on a call, so I'm going to have to take you to her. You can stay with her until she's through."

Any other time Jaime would have leapt at the chance to make a call with his Aunt Sam, but at the moment, roping steer heads with Jesse held a greater appeal. "Ah, Mama, can't I stay by myself? I don't need no baby-sitter."

"*Any* baby-sitter," she corrected automatically. "And no, you can't stay by yourself. I'd only worry." She motioned impatiently for him to join her. "Come on, now. I'm already running late."

"I could stay with the boy," Jesse offered.

Though she'd hoped to ignore his presence, Mandy was forced to acknowledge Jesse, though she did so without sparing him a glance. "Thanks, but I couldn't ask you to waste any more of your time with Jaime. He's monopolized enough of your day as it is."

Jesse stepped forward, placing himself between Jaime and Mandy, forcing her to look at him. The fact that her heart tripped into a faster beat at the sight of him only proved to her that she was right in trying to avoid him.

"You didn't ask," he murmured. "I offered. And it's my time to waste." Ignoring the stubborn gleam in Mandy's eyes, Jesse turned to look at Jaime over his shoulder. "How about it, Jaime? Are you willing to put up with me until your Aunt Sam gets home?"

The beaming smile on Jaime's face was answer enough. "Hey, cool! We can practice my roping a little longer."

Knowing that arguing would do no good and would only make Jaime curious about her reluctance to leave him with Jesse, Mandy tried to accept defeat as graciously as possible. "Thank you. Sam shouldn't be too much longer. Dinner's in the oven. There's plenty for the two of you." She stepped around Jesse and went to Jaime, smoothing a loving hand over his unruly hair.

He immediately ducked from beneath the motherly gesture. "Ah, Mama," he complained as he trudged for the steer head to reclaim his rope.

Mandy let her hand fall limply to her side, saddened that her son was outgrowing her displays of affection. "You mind Jesse and do what he says," she called after him.

"Yes, ma'am," he muttered.

"And don't forget to shower before you go to bed."

"Yeah, yeah," he grumbled.

With no other instructions left to offer, reluctantly Mandy turned back to Jesse. He stood facing her, his hat shoved far back on his head, his hands braced at his hips. His lips were thinned and, in spite of her earlier decision to avoid him, she found herself wanting to press a finger there to soften their tightness, to place her own lips there and sip the anger away.

Immediately, she dropped her gaze, focusing instead on an invisible fleck of dust on her skirt and brushing at it with fingers that hungered to do other things. "In case Sam should be late, his bedtime is ten."

"Yes, ma'am."

At the sarcasm in his voice, Mandy snapped her head back up. "I didn't mean to sound as if I were giving orders," she said defensively. "I was only trying to acquaint you with his schedule."

"It's a damn shame I have to be told my own son's bedtime."

Horrified that Jaime might have overheard Jesse's comment, Mandy quickly looked toward her son. But Jaime was busy practicing his throw and thankfully not paying attention to the conversation going on behind him.

She turned back to Jesse, setting her jaw as she took a threatening step closer. "Don't you dare take advantage of my being gone and tell him you're his father," she warned in a low voice. "If you do, I swear I'll arrange it so that you'll never lay eyes on him again."

Jesse just stared at her, his gaze never once wavering. "Are you trying to threaten me, Mandy?"

"No," she said tightly. "It's just a warning you'd be wise to heed."

One side of Jesse's mouth curled in a sardonic smile. "Your warning is duly noted." When she started to step around him, he shifted, blocking her way. She snapped her gaze to his.

He took his eyes on a slow journey down the front of her, taking in the sage-green Western-style skirt, matching blouse and colorfully stitched Western boots. "Nice outfit," he murmured. He hooked a finger in the V of her collarless blouse and drew her closer. She stiffened, the gold in her green eyes sparking fire. "You have fun now, you hear?" he murmured huskily. "And don't worry about a thing," he added as he dragged his knuckle up the smooth column of her neck. "Jaime and I'll get along just fine."

Mandy jerked away from him and wheeled for the house, her skin on fire. Behind her, she heard Jesse's soft chuckling.

Jaime was still throwing lassos at the steer when the sound of a car coming up the drive made Jesse glance back over his shoulder. His attention now on the low-slung sports car racing up the drive, he passed the rope he'd just gathered into a coil back to Jaime. "Give it another try," he murmured.

He watched the car squeal to a stop in front of the ranch house, spitting gravel from behind its rear tires. The driver's door swung open, a hand shot out and slapped the car's roof as a bear of a man used it as a brace to propel himself up and out of the car's cramped interior.

"Hellfire," Jesse muttered under his breath, immediately recognizing the thick neck, the wide shoulders, the muscled arms and thighs of John Lee Carter. "What's he doing here?"

Jaime dropped the lasso and turned to look. "Oh, that's John Lee Carter. He and Mama have a date tonight."

At that moment Mandy skipped down the front porch steps and stood on tiptoe to plant a kiss on John Lee's cheek. Laughing, she looped an arm through his and walked with him to the other side of the car, where he opened the door and guided her inside.

Jesse wasn't prepared for the jealousy that slammed

into him at the sight of Mandy with another man. It burned through his veins, curling his hands into fists at his sides.

"He used to play professional football," Jaime offered, moving to Jesse's side. "But he blew out a knee and had to retire."

Yeah, Jesse had read about that. But nothing he'd read had said anything about John Lee moving back home and certainly nothing about Mandy being coupled with him. There'd been plenty of mentions of models and actresses and something about an affair with a princess that was quickly hushed up. But nothing, ever, about Mandy.

Jaime stole a look at Jesse's face, hoping to plant the seed of an idea that he'd been pondering for the last few days. "Mama sure does look pretty, doesn't she?"

Jesse curled his nose in disgust, refusing to answer. The sage-green silk skirt and matching blouse he'd admired earlier, suddenly lost its appeal when he realized it was John Lee she'd worn it for.

John Lee Carter was way too experienced for Mandy, he told himself. A relationship with a womanizer like him would only end with Mandy getting hurt. And Jesse wasn't about to let anyone hurt Mandy. She'd suffered enough at the hands of her father. Jesse had already taken one step toward the house to send John Lee packing, when he realized what he was doing.

On a muffled curse, he snatched the rope from Jaime's hand, swung it in a fast whirring circle over his head and let it fly. The lasso dropped dead center over the steer's head and Jesse gave the rope a jerk with enough anger behind it to have the bale rearing and toppling over backwards.

"Wow!" Jaime breathed. "Can you teach me to do *that?*"

Jesse paced in front of the window, stopping occasionally to shoot a furious glance at the dark drive beyond. When nothing moved beyond the panes of glass to disturb the night, cursing, he'd swing back into his angry pacing.

Sam had called shortly after Jaime had gone to bed to tell Jesse that she was going to have to spend the night with a sick horse and asked if he minded staying with Jaime until Mandy returned home. Of course he hadn't minded staying with Jaime, but he *did* resent the hell out of the fact that it was now pushing one and there wasn't a sign of Mandy!

"Where the hell is she?" he muttered under his breath as he jerked the drapes to the side for another look outside. But the only thing he saw were the same visions that had taunted him for the last hour: images of John Lee and Mandy, naked, their arms locked tight around each other in a passionate embrace while they rolled wildly on some giant-size bed custom-designed to fit John Lee's muscular frame.

As he stared blindly out the window, the vision gave way to twin spots of light that grew larger and brighter until Jesse recognized the sports car's dark, sleek shape. The car roared to a stop in front of the house in the same way it had arrived earlier—squealing tires and spitting gravel. Jesse dropped the drape in disgust. "About damned time she came dragging home," he muttered as he snatched his hat off the entry table and rammed it on his head.

Mandy came in on a rush of air, her cheeks flushed, her hair mussed, and a smile on her face. It wilted somewhat when her gaze met Jesse's accusing one. "Oh," she said dully. "I thought Sam would be here by now."

"She called. She has to spend the night with a sick horse. She asked me if I'd stay until you got back."

Mandy tossed her purse to the entry hall table. "I'm back, so you're free to go."

Though that's exactly what Jesse had been planning to do, at her casual dismissal he found himself squaring off in front of her, his hands fisted at his hips. "What the hell do you think you're doing hanging out all night with the likes of John Lee Carter?"

That he would dare to question how late she stayed out, and with whom, had Mandy tipping up her chin. "John Lee is a friend of mine, and at one time a friend of yours, too—or have you forgotten that?"

"I haven't forgotten a damn thing, least of all John Lee's wild ways."

"And exactly what are you insinuating?"

"Look at you!" Jesse said thrusting a hand at her. "You look like you just crawled out of bed, for God's sake!"

Heat flamed in Mandy's cheeks. Though her present state of disarray was a result of John Lee putting the top down on his car, Mandy refused to explain that to Jesse. John Lee was a friend of hers, a good friend, and that was all, but she refused to explain that to Jesse, either. Gathering the silky fabric of her skirt in her fingers, she tried to hold on to her temper. "What I do and who I choose to do it with, is no concern of yours."

"Like hell it's not," he muttered as he ripped off his hat and sent it sailing across the room. In two long strides he'd closed the distance between them and had her in his arms, determined to wipe the look of defiance from her lips. He crushed his mouth over hers, stifling her cry of refusal.

Mandy flattened her hands against his chest, intending to push him away. But instead, her traitorous fingers curled into his shirt's fabric and clung.

With a punishing cruelty that he knew he had no right to inflict, Jesse stabbed his tongue between her lips...but all he tasted was sweetness, innocence...and a heat that had nothing to do with anger and everything to do with the passion that surged to life between Mandy and him now.

"Tell me he means nothing to you," he demanded as he left her lips and moved against the smooth column of her neck. "Tell me he didn't touch you like this." While his hands locked behind her waist, bowing her body to his, his lips burned a trail of fire down her throat. He warmed a silk-covered breast with his breath, then closed his mouth over it, heating her flesh through the thin fabric and drawing her nipple into a hard knot of desire.

"No," she whispered, lifting her hands to tangle in his hair, helpless to give him anything but the truth. "There's never been anyone but you."

Fired by the admission, Jesse nosed the blouse's fabric aside and caught the budded nipple between his teeth, eliciting a cry from Mandy. Her fingers dug into his scalp. "Jesse. Oh, Jesse!" she cried helplessly.

He released his hold on her long enough to find one of the silver buttons that lined the front of her blouse. He managed to free one, then in frustration gave a vicious yank and the rest popped free. Buttons clicked against the tiled floor and rolled and spun unheeded while her blouse fell open, fully exposing her breasts to his hungry eyes. Shoving his hands beneath the fabric, he jerked the blouse off her shoulders and down her arms, then twisted the fabric at her wrists, trapping her hands in silk bonds behind her.

His eyes met hers, and Mandy sucked in a breath at the wildness, at the heat she saw there before he dipped his head and closed his mouth again over her breast, this time drawing her deep inside. Pleasure shot through her, stabbing low in her abdomen and quivering there like a well-aimed arrow. She threw back her head, arching hard against him, straining against the silk bonds. But with her hands entangled behind her, she could do nothing to relieve the aching need to touch him as well.

"Jesse, please," she whimpered.

"Please what?" he demanded against her flesh.

"Please, let me touch you."

He lifted his head, his brown eyes burning into hers. In answer, he tugged the silk from her wrists and tossed the blouse aside, but before she could lift her hands to him, he caught her up in his arms. "Where's your room?"

"No," she cried, wagging her head. "Not there. Jaime might—"

"Where, then?"

"The barn," she whispered. "We'll be safe there."

Five

Mandy buried her face in Jesse's neck, her hot breath searing his skin. "The trainer's room," she whispered as he paused inside the barn. When he continued to hesitate, she lifted a hand, pointing to the closed door beside the lab.

Using his boot, Jesse kicked open the door, strode inside, then caught the door with his heel and closed it behind them. A thin thread of moonlight streamed through a high window, illuminating a small cot in its narrow beam. Without breaking stride, Jesse crossed to it and laid Mandy on the bed.

Stepping back, he stared down at her, sweeping his gaze over her flushed face, her swollen lips, her breasts that seemed to swell beneath his gaze. "Who do you see?" he whispered, emotion making his accent heavy. "Who do you want?"

A sob caught in Mandy's throat. "You, Jesse. Only you."

Seemingly satisfied with her response, he reached down, caught her heel and tugged off first one boot, then the other, and dropped them to the floor. Shifting his gaze to hers, he caught the elastic waistband of her skirt and dragged it down her legs, taking her panty hose with it. He tossed both carelessly to the floor before picking up her foot again and cradling it between his strong hands. His thumbs moved in mindless, intoxicating circles across the arch of her foot, until her breath came in deep gulps. Dropping to a knee at the foot of the bed, he replaced his thumbs with his mouth and pressed his lips to the sensitive skin there before sweeping his tongue along the length of her arch.

Heat raced up Mandy's leg and swirled in a churning pool of desire between her legs. Lifting her hands above her head, she grabbed for the bed's metal frame and clung, squeezing her eyes shut against the pain and pleasure that surged through her in crashing waves. When she was sure she couldn't bear any more, his lips smoothed upwards, slowly, over her ankle, pausing to nip at a muscled calf, higher still to wet her thigh with his tongue while his hands kneaded at heated flesh. To Mandy it was torture. The sweetest torture she'd ever known.

At the juncture of her thighs, he paused again, lifting his head to meet her questioning gaze. Watching her, his own eyes guarded, he cupped her feminine nest and squeezed. Instinctively, she bucked against his hand.

"Jesse," she whispered desperately. "Please."

In answer, he stood, toed off his boots, stripped off his socks, then reached for the top button on his shirt.

Mandy pushed herself to a sitting position, reaching for him. "No, let me."

When he dropped his arms to his sides, she swung her legs over the side of the bed, lifted her hands and freed each button, her fingers shaking uncontrollably. Every brush of her fingertips against his skin sent Jesse's pulse racing faster and faster, until his chest heaved with each drawn breath. Nearly crazy with his need for her, he grabbed for his belt buckle, flipped it open and shucked off his jeans. Leaning over her, he forced her back to the bed and followed her down.

Bracing his hands on either side of her face, he held her with his gaze. "You're mine, Mandy," he told her even as he lowered his head over hers to seal his claim. Their lips touched once, twice, then, with a groan, Jesse collapsed on top of her and flipped over, taking her with him, until she lay on top of him.

His hands cupped her bottom, guiding her to him. At the first thrust of his swollen manhood, Mandy arched, bracing her hands against his chest, taking him even deeper.

"Mine," Jesse repeated through gritted teeth. "Always mine."

"Yes," Mandy gasped as the first wave took her. "Ye-esss!" she cried as she felt the heat of his passion jet through her, sending her spinning crazily over the edge.

Mandy awakened slowly, gradually becoming aware of the dull ache that throbbed between her legs and smiled softly at the memory of its cause. Rolling to her back, she scraped her still damp hair from her face. "Jesse?"

When he didn't answer, she lifted herself on one

elbow and looked around the shadowed room. A vise slowly tightened around her chest. He was gone. He'd left without saying so much as a goodbye.

Fighting back the sting of rejection, she slipped from the narrow cot, gathered her skirt from the floor and stepped into it. Remembering that her blouse still lay on the entry-hall floor, she dropped back down onto the cot, giving in to the tears that burned her eyes. "Oh, Jesse," she sobbed, dropping her face into her hands. "How could you do this to me?"

But in her heart, she knew she shared part of the blame. He'd only taken what she'd freely offered. But had he taken her in the same spirit with which she'd given herself to him? With love?

Shaking her head, she rose, scraping the heels of her hands beneath her eyes...and saw his blue shirt draped across the foot of the bed. Fresh tears welled as she realized he'd left it for her. She picked up the shirt and slipped her arms through the sleeves, drawing the collar to her nose. Inhaling deeply, she breathed in his scent. On a shuddery sigh, she stooped, gathered up her boots and quietly stole from the room.

Once outside the barn, she gathered the plackets of his shirt tighter around her and ran through the fading darkness, anxious to get back to the house before her wranglers rose for the day and caught her sneaking from the barn half-dressed. Inside the dark kitchen, she set her boots down and turned to close the door quietly behind her.

"Mandy?"

Mandy jumped and whirled, flattening her back against the door, to find Sam standing in the triangle of light cast from the open refrigerator door. She placed a hand over her heart. "Sam! You scared the life out of me."

"Sorry." Sam closed the refrigerator and took a sip of the milk she'd just poured, her eyes widening above the glass's rim when she saw how Mandy was dressed. Slowly she lowered the glass. "Am I to assume that John Lee is wearing your blouse, since you are wearing his shirt?"

Mandy felt her cheeks burn in embarrassment. "It isn't John Lee's," she murmured and stepped around her sister to open the refrigerator again.

Sam moved to peer over the door at the top of Mandy's head. "Well, whose is it, then?"

"Jesse's."

The name came from the depths of the refrigerator, but Sam heard the mumbled confession. "Jesse's!" she repeated, shocked.

Mandy stepped back, a pitcher of juice in her hand, and closed the door, turning to face her sister, her eyes brimming with tears. "Yes, Jesse's."

Sam immediately set her glass of milk aside and caught Mandy by the shoulders. "Did he hurt you?"

Mandy wagged her head, giving in to the tears. "No, he—" She stopped, unable to explain what had happened between them. "No, he didn't hurt me," she finally managed to say. She lifted her face to her sister's. "Oh, Sam, I still love him," she sobbed brokenly.

Sam gathered her close in a hug. "I know," she murmured soothingly. "I know."

Once the floodgates had opened, Mandy was incapable of stopping the flow of words that poured forth. "When I came home tonight, he was waiting for me and he started yelling at me for staying out so late.

Then, the next thing I knew, he had me in his arms and he was kissing me." She paused to draw in a shuddery breath, then plunged on. "I w-wanted to make him stop, b-but I couldn't," she sobbed. "I *wanted* him to make love to me. I've wanted him to since the day he brought Jaime home."

Though the subject was an uncomfortable one for Sam, Mandy knew, her sister listened, patting and soothing. "So you did?" Sam asked uneasily.

"Yes. In the barn." Mandy pushed from Sam's embrace, tears of frustration streaming down her face. "But when I woke up, he was gone," she cried. "He left without saying a word."

Unsure what was expected of her, Sam asked carefully, "And what did you want him to say?"

Mandy whirled away, shoving the pitcher of juice onto the counter. She planted her hands against the cool tiles as she stared blindly out at the pinkening sky beyond the kitchen window. "I don't know," she mumbled miserably.

Sam stepped up behind her, laying a comforting hand on Mandy's shoulder. "Maybe he left because he didn't know what to say," she offered gently. "Maybe this is as confusing for him as it is for you."

A shudder moved Mandy's shoulders beneath Sam's hands. "No, I think it's more than that," she murmured as if to herself. "It's almost as if he wants to punish me in some way."

"For keeping Jaime from him?"

"Partly," Mandy replied slowly, only now beginning to understand the anger behind Jesse's passion. "But more because I didn't leave with him years ago when he asked me to. I don't think he's ever forgiven me for that."

"Have you forgiven him for leaving without you?" Sam asked pointedly.

Mandy turned, lifting her gaze to Sam's. "I don't know," she said sadly as she turned away. "I just don't know."

By the time Mandy crawled into her own bed to catch a few hours of sleep, Jesse was well on the way to being roaring drunk. After leaving her in the barn, he'd driven back to the Circle Bar and dug Pete's fifth of whiskey from the tack box where his old friend had always kept his secret stash hidden.

Sprawled on the floor, Jesse shifted his shoulders against the rough barn wall, oblivious to the splinters that dug into his bare back as he lifted the bottle to his lips. The whiskey burned a path down his throat and Jesse shuddered, then growled as he dragged his wrist across his mouth.

He never should have touched her, he told himself for the hundredth time in less than two hours. He should have left the minute she walked in the door. And would have, he assured himself, if she hadn't looked like she'd just crawled out of John Lee's bed. Snarling as the image formed, he lifted the bottle again and took an angry swig.

Flushed cheeks, mussed hair, wearing a smile that looked a little too satisfied to please him. He snorted, setting the bottle on the plank floor near his raised knee. No, he couldn't leave then. Not without first kissing that sexy mouth. Not without giving her something to remember him by.

A smug smile curled at his lips. Yeah, he'd given her something to think about, all right. She'd all but begged him to make love to her. By the time they'd made it to the barn, she'd been hot and primed for nobody but him. And when she'd fallen asleep in his arms, it had been *his* name on her lips—Jesse's. He'd punished her, just as he'd intended to.

If that's the case, then why are you drinking yourself into a blind stupor?

He frowned at the far wall, not liking his conscience's question. Because he liked the taste, he told himself, and took another long swig to prove it.

Yeah, and you're going to like the taste of that headache in the morning, too. Why don't you just face the facts, amigo, *you're still in love with the woman.*

Jesse's fingers tightened on the bottle's slim neck. He didn't love her, he told himself. He hated her. She'd lied to him. She'd whispered promises of love and marriage and spending eternity together, then turned her back on him when her old man had made her choose between her Mexican lover and her father. And she'd kept their son from him for twelve years. Reason enough to hate her. And certainly reason enough for him to seek his own form of revenge from her.

Revenge? Was that what you were seeking? Is that what you were thinking about when you held her in your arms while she slept?

Jesse bristled at the memory. Yeah, he assured himself, that's exactly what he was seeking.

So why are you rubbing your hand over your heart?

Jesse glanced down, only then becoming aware of the unconscious gesture and the ache beneath it. With a resigned sigh, he raised his other knee, lowering his arm to rest on it. He dropped his head down between his elbows. "Because it hurts," he muttered miserably. "After all these years, it still hurts."

* * *

From the kitchen window, Margo watched Jesse stagger from the barn to a water trough beside the corral. He stooped, bracing his hands on either side of the trough, and ducked his head into the water. He rose seconds later, gasping, dragging his hands through his dripping hair, while water ran in rivulets down his bare back.

Drunk, Margo thought in disgust. How like him. And where had he been all night, anyway? She knew for a fact that he hadn't returned home before two because she'd watched for him until then.

"That McCloud slut," Margo muttered under her breath. "I'll bet *that's* who he's been spending all his time with."

Later that morning, Margo parked her Lincoln Town Car by the gasoline pump at the crossing of the two state highways that intersected the ranching community, then pressed a manicured nail to a button and lowered the tinted window. In the bay opposite her, a truck bearing the logo of the Double-Cross Heart Ranch was parked. A cowboy stood beside it, pumping gas, his back braced against the truck's cab, watching her from beneath the brim of a sweat-stained hat.

"Do you have any news for me?" she said, keeping her voice low so as to keep their conversation private.

The cowboy flicked the nozzle's metal lever into place, setting it on automatic, then stepped over the concrete island that separated them. "Maybe," he said, leaning to brace his forearms along the open window. He grinned, revealing a row of tobacco-stained teeth as crooked as the smile he offered her.

Repulsed by the sight and the accompanying odor that wafted through the window, Margo drew away.

Frowning, she dipped a hand into her purse and drew out a folded bill. She pressed it into the cowboy's hand.

He studied it a moment. "Seems like the information I have should be worth more than a measly fifty bucks." He shifted his gaze to hers, his eyes turning dark and menacing. "A rich woman like you could surely come up with a little more than this."

"Oh, for heaven's sake," Margo muttered disagreeably, but dipped her hand into her bag again and slapped a matching bill into his greedy palm. "But that's all. Not a cent more."

Grinning, the cowboy stuffed the bills into his shirt pocket. "He's there all right," he told her. "Comes almost every day. Says he's there to break a stallion, but if you ask me, he's spending more time with the boss's son than he does with that crazy horse."

Margo managed to keep her expression free of the anger the news drew. "What about the McCloud woman? Is he spending any time with her?"

The cowboy shook his head. "If you're askin' me if he's beddin' her, I cain't rightly say."

"Can't or won't?" Margo snapped impatiently.

"Cain't," he repeated. "Course, I do require some sleep. They might be slippin' off while I'm catchin' me some shut-eye and I'd never be the wiser."

Margo thinned her lips. "I'm not paying you to sleep. I'm paying you to provide information."

"Yessum, that you are," he agreed with a nod.

With a huff of breath, Margo shifted the car into drive. "When you have something worthwhile to report, you know how to reach me."

The cowboy stepped back as the car peeled from the bay. "Yessum, I surely do," he murmured, grinning.

* * *

The drum Jesse had awakened to kept up its relentless pounding throughout the morning while he worked Judas around the arena. He'd managed to get a halter on the stallion and had clamped a longe line to its ring, keeping the opposite end of the line gripped tightly in his gloved hand. He urged the horse forward with the snap of a long whip, which he dragged across the ground as he slowly turned, keeping himself even with the horse's movements.

Sweat soaked his back and stung his eyes, but he refused to stop, knowing that only time would silence the drum in his head and cure him of his hangover.

"Hey, Jesse!"

Jesse winced at Jaime's loud shout, but didn't take his eyes off the stallion. "Over here," he called back.

Behind him, he heard Jaime's boots clatter up the rails of the corral. "Where've you been hiding all morning?" he asked the boy.

"Doin' my chores."

Jesse heard the loathing behind his son's muttered response and grinned, shooting a quick look at Jaime over his shoulder. "All done?"

"Yep. Even remembered to take out the kitchen trash." Jaime slapped his hands to his knees and leaned forward, nearly losing his balance on the top rail. "Hey! You got a halter on him!" he exclaimed.

"Yep," Jesse replied, mimicking his son's response. "He's still like a stick of dynamite, ready to go off at any second, but at least he's following my commands."

"Are you gonna ride him today?"

"No, it's too soon yet." Keeping a watchful eye on the stallion, Jesse gave the rope a sharp tug, calling "Whoa!" Judas danced a few steps, straining against the line, but Jesse dug in his heels, bracing himself, and the stallion stopped, muscles quivering.

"Easy, boy," he murmured as he took a step toward the horse. Judas turned his head to watch him, his eyes rolling wildly. "Easy now," Jesse continued to soothe as he held out a hand. The stallion jerked his head back and tried to rear. Again Jesse planted his feet, dropping the whip to take the line in both hands. But he was powerless against the animal's strength.

The horse reared again, this time succeeding, and had Jesse hurtling through the air. Jesse landed on his knees just as Judas spun, kicking out with his rear legs. The stallion landed a blow to the side of Jesse's head and one to his back, knocking the breath from him, before galloping to the far side of the arena.

"Jesse!"

Jesse heard Jaime's cry of fear just before the darkness took him.

"Is he gonna be okay?"

Jesse heard the uncertainty in Jaime's whispered question but couldn't find the strength to reassure his son. Flat on his back, his eyes closed against the pain, he struggled just to breathe.

Fingertips, soft and soothing, fluttered at his brow. *Mandy's?*

"He's going to be just fine. You'll see."

Yes, the voice told him that it was Mandy caring for him. But below the reassuring tone, Jesse heard her own doubts and he knew he had to put both their fears to rest. But as hard as he tried, he couldn't open his eyes, much less form the words necessary to reassure them.

"Go to the house and get me the ice pack from the

freezer.'' Jaime must have hesitated, because Mandy added more firmly, "Now, Jaime. We need the ice for this lump on his head."

Jesse heard a door open and close softly, then silence. The fingertips returned, smoothing his hair back from his forehead.

"Jesse?" she whispered. "Jesse? Can you hear me?"

He tried to open his eyes, but the glare of sunlight streaming from the window over his head made him slam them shut again...but not before he caught a glimpse of where he was. The trainer's room. On the narrow cot that he had shared with Mandy the night before.

On a groan, he lifted a weak hand, meaning to brush her hand away, but found himself catching her fingers in his and clinging weakly. "Yeah," he croaked. "I hear you."

"Do you remember what happened?"

Jesse frowned, then winced when the pounding kicked up its tempo in his head at the movement. He remembered Judas rearing, then falling. And he remembered the blinding pain when Judas's hoof had connected with his head. But after that, everything was a little fuzzy.

"Most of it," he replied and felt her sigh of relief against his cheek. "How'd I get in here?"

"Gabe and some of the hands slipped a board under you and carried you here." She squeezed her fingers around his hand. "Can you move?" she asked.

He tried to lift his head and winced when the room began to spin. He dropped his head back to the cot with a low moan. "I don't think so. Not yet, anyway."

"Does it feel as if anything is broken?"

He frowned, concentrating hard on the pain. "No. I don't think so."

"There's a good-size lump on your head and a superficial scrape at your temple. What else hurts?"

"My back."

"Do you think you can roll over far enough for me to see?"

She was being so kind, so gentle, and Jesse couldn't help but wonder why, considering how he'd treated her the night before. He opened his eyes, squinting to meet her gaze. The worry he saw in her eyes sent a fresh wave of shame washing through him. How could she be so kind, when he had been so cruel? Uncomfortable with looking at her, he released her hand to clasp the side of the cot, easing himself onto his side. With care, Mandy pulled his shirt from the waistband of his jeans and tried to lift the hem. "We're going to have to take this off," she murmured.

Jesse moved his hand to the row of pearlized snaps that lined the front of his shirt and gave a tug. They popped open and Mandy gingerly eased the sleeve down his arm and laid open his shirt, exposing his back.

She sucked in a startled breath at the sight that greeted her. "Oh, Jesse!" she cried, touching a tentative finger to the small of his back where the perfect impression of Judas's hoof lay. Blood was already clotted on the horseshoe-shaped wound.

"Is it bad?"

Mandy swallowed hard. "I'm not sure. I'll need to clean it first." She quickly turned, picking up a bottle of peroxide from the supplies she'd laid out on the table beside the bed, then tipped it over his back, letting the liquid flush the wound.

Jesse flinched, sucking in air through his teeth.

"I'm sorry," she murmured as she dabbed with a square of gauze. "Does it sting?"

"No," he managed to get out. "It's cold."

Mandy bit back a smile. "Cold won't hurt you."

"I think I'm the best judge of that," he muttered dryly.

As the blood and dirt disappeared, Mandy saw that the cut wasn't deep, but was already swelling and turning blue. A good sign, she hoped. "We need to get you to the hospital."

Jesse tested the bump on his head with a tentative hand, unsure if the drums that continued to beat there were a result of the fifth of whiskey he'd consumed the night before or of Judas's well-aimed kick. "No hospital," he decided. "It's just a graze."

"Jesse—" Mandy began.

"No. I don't want some sawbones poking at me."

Mandy let out a frustrated breath. "You're being stubborn. You need to see a doctor."

"I know when a doctor's required. Pete can take care of me once I get home." He started to roll to his back again, but Mandy thrust a hand against his spine, stopping him.

"At least let me put a bandage on the wound to keep it clean."

Though Jesse wanted off the bed and out of the trainer's room, he decided the fastest way to accomplish that might be to let her do what she wanted. "Okay, but make it fast."

Frowning, Mandy pulled a fresh square of gauze from the box. After liberally dosing the wound with antibiotic, she placed the gauze over it, then taped the bandage into place. As she started to turn away, she caught a glimpse of another scrape and turned back. Leaning closer, she touched a finger to first one red welt, then another. "Jesse! You've got splinters all over your back."

He tensed, remembering the barn's rough wall that had cut into his back when he'd been working on drowning his troubles with whiskey. "It's nothing," he said, as her fingers trailed over his back. "Pete'll pull 'em out."

But her fingers continued to move across his back, and Jesse closed his eyes against the feel of them, trying his best to shut out memories of those same hands roaming and caressing his back the night before.

Unable to do so, he tried to sit up, but Mandy pushed him right back down.

"Pete is bound to be pushing sixty and probably blind as a bat," she argued. "He'd never be able to see these splinters to remove them. I have some tweezers right here. It won't take me a minute to pull them out for you."

Smothering a groan against the biceps that supported his cheek, Jesse closed his eyes again, knowing it was useless to argue. But the feel of her fingers on his back was as unsettling as being in the trainer's room with her, lying on the bed where they'd made love. He wanted out in the worst sort of way.

The door squeaked open behind him.

"Hey, you're awake!"

Jaime's face appeared in front of Jesse's. Jesse managed a lopsided smile. "Yeah, I'm awake."

Jaime lifted his gaze to his mother's face. "What're you doin'?"

Her lips firmed in concentration, Mandy murmured, "I'm pulling splinters out of his back."

"Splinters?" Jaime dropped his gaze to Jesse's, his eyebrows knitted together. "How'd you get splinters in your back?"

Jesse felt his cheeks warm. "I—uh—"

Mandy leaned over him, saving him from having to answer, and took the ice pack from Jaime's hands. The feel of her abdomen pressed against his spine left a square of heat that did everything but shut down Jesse's breathing entirely.

She laid the pack against the lump on his head. "Jaime," she instructed, "put your hand right here and hold this in place."

Jaime did so, grinning at Jesse. "She's pretty bossy, isn't she?" he whispered.

Jesse craned his head to look over his shoulder and frown at Mandy. "Yeah, she is." Then yelped when Mandy tugged out another splinter.

"Oh, for goodness' sake!" she exclaimed. "That couldn't have hurt that badly." She dipped her head closer, frowning, and tested another splinter with a fingernail. "How *did* you manage to get splinters in your back?"

Jesse heaved a frustrated breath, then decided the best way to avoid answering the question might be to put the heat on Mandy. "Well, you see, I left my shirt in—"

Immediately, Mandy jackknifed upright. "It isn't important," she interrupted, and grabbed for the bottle of peroxide. She splashed some across the scraped skin where splinters had once been embedded, hoping to shush him. She didn't want her son to hear that Jesse had left his shirt in the trainer's room for her to wear.

Jesse sucked in a shocked breath as the cold liquid hit his back. "Damn it! You might've warned me first,'' he yelled crossly. He caught the gleam of a wicked smile on his son's face and released the breath on a sigh. ''Sorry. Didn't mean to cuss in front of you.''

''Oh, that's all right,'' Jaime assured him. ''Mama's let loose with a few that would burn your ears.''

Mandy reared back, looking at her son in dismay. ''Jaime McCloud! I have not.''

Jaime pushed his hands to his knees and stood. ''Yeah, you have.'' He grinned a mischievous grin at her across the width of the bed. ''You just didn't know I was in hearing distance.''

Her cheeks flaming, Mandy started gathering up supplies. ''I've removed all the splinters I can see. You can go now, Jesse.''

Relieved to be free at last, Jesse rolled to his back and then into a sitting position on the side of the bed, all in one smooth move. Nausea churned in his stomach and rose to burn his throat while the room spun crazily around him. Groaning, he dipped his head between his knees, grabbing his head with his hands to keep it from falling off.

Mandy was on her knees in front of him, her hand on his shoulder, before he drew the first ragged breath. ''What's wrong?''

''It's nothing…really. I must have just moved too fast.''

She stood, but kept her hand on his shoulder to keep him from falling all the way to the floor. ''You've probably got a concussion. Jaime,'' she ordered firmly, ''go and find Gabe and tell him to come and help us move Jesse to the house.''

Jesse jerked up his head to tell her he wasn't going to her house, but back to the Circle Bar where he belonged, then quickly dropped it again when a fresh wave of nausea rose. "No," he gasped. "Just help me get to my truck. I can make it back to the Circle Bar."

"And kill yourself in the process," Mandy muttered irritably. She waved her son away with an impatient hand. "Now hurry and find Gabe. We need to get Jesse into bed."

Six

Jesse opened his eyes and blinked several times, trying to get a bead on his location. Shadows moved, dancing away from the moonlight that leaked through the window at his left. Squinting, he was able to make out a dressing table on one wall, a dresser on another…and a feminine, flowery scent that hung in the air just beneath his nose.

What the hell?

Then he remembered. Groaning, he closed his eyes again. He was at the Double-Cross. But not for long, he promised himself. He rolled to sit on the side of the bed, gripping the edge of the mattress with both hands until his head stopped spinning. Once he was sure he could do so without falling, he stood and reached for his jeans, which someone had thought to hook over the bottom post of the bed. Pulling them on, he caught sight of his boots propped on the floor in front of the dresser. Without bothering to zip his jeans, he strode across the room and stooped to hook two fingers in the top of them.

And the dang room started spinning again.

Bracing a hand against the glass-topped dresser to keep from falling over, he straightened a little and found himself face-to-face with a picture of Mandy. With the moonlight behind him, throwing a glare on the picture, Jesse couldn't make out the details of the image. Casting a cautious glance over his shoulder to make sure no one was watching, he picked it up for a closer inspection.

In the picture Mandy sat in a rocker with a baby settled against her breasts, a radiant smile lighting her face. The sight of the infant's cherubic face drove a stake, hot and searing, straight through Jesse's chest. He reeled, bumping his hip against the dresser to support himself as he clutched the frame in his hands.

Jaime? He touched a finger to the infant's face. *My son.* Taking the picture, he staggered back to the bed and flipped on the lamp beside it before dropping down on the mattress.

As he stared at the photo, tears burned his throat. He'd never thought of Jaime as an infant before. His only association with his son was with the twelve-year-old version of the boy he'd met on that first day by the lake on the Circle Bar. Tears blurred the infant's image as Jesse was confronted with all the years, all the growing he'd missed.

"Jesse?"

He snapped up his head at the sound of Mandy's voice to find her standing in the doorway, watching him, the collar of her robe clutched in one white-knuckled fist at her breasts.

He lifted the frame, then let it drop to rest on his knee. "I didn't mean to pry. I was getting my boots and I saw the picture. I—" He shook his head, overcome with emotion.

Mandy stepped into the room and crossed to him, uncertain what was going on.

Jesse lifted his head to look at her. "I never knew him like this," he said, his voice thick with tears. "He was so tiny, so fragile-looking."

Mandy sank down to the bed beside him, her heart breaking for Jesse. "Yes, he was. He only weighed seven pounds and six ounces when he was born." She eased the picture from Jesse's hands and lifted it, smiling as she remembered. "But he had the thickest head of black hair you've ever seen. And the bluest eyes."

Jesse cocked his head to look at her. "Blue? But his eyes are green. Like yours."

Mandy laughed softly. "Yes. Now they are. But when he was a baby, they were the color of a summer sky."

Jesse took the picture from her and stared long and hard at it. "I missed so much."

Mandy heard the regret in his voice, and the fissure in her heart widened a fraction more. She'd had Jaime from the moment of his birth, but Jesse hadn't had that precious gift. "I have albums and albums of pictures," she offered softly. "Would you like to see them?"

Without lifting his gaze from the picture he still held, Jesse murmured, "Yes, I'd like that very much."

Going to her closet, Mandy lifted down several albums from a shelf and returned to the bed. She set all the albums to the side but one, then opened it across her knees, smoothing her hand across the page. "These pictures were taken at the hospital where he was born."

"Back east," Jesse said without thinking.

Mandy looked at him in surprise. "How did you know that?"

Jesse heaved a shuddery breath. "Pete told me. He said Lucas sent you away when he found out you were pregnant."

Mandy dropped her chin to her chest, focusing on the page of pictures once again, but unable to see them through the tears that sprinted to her eyes. "Yes, he did. He sent me to my Aunt Mildred's in Raleigh."

Jesse reached over and covered her hand with his. "I'm sorry, Mandy. I know how much that must have hurt—"

She shook her head slowly. "It doesn't matter anymore." Sniffing back the tears, she pointed to a picture. "See that mop of hair? All the nurses in the hospital said Jaime was the most beautiful baby they'd ever seen."

"Handsome," Jesse corrected. "Girls are beautiful. Boys are handsome."

Mandy laughed softly. "No, Jaime was beautiful." She turned the page. "Here he is at Aunt Mildred's, suffering through his first bath."

Jesse eased closer for a better look and his shoulder brushed Mandy's. Neither moved away from the contact. "His face is as red as a tomato."

"He hated baths, even then." She turned another page and then another, sharing Jaime's life with Jesse, if only through the medium of pictures. With each flip of a page, a bond slowly grew between them, tying them together, formed by the son they'd created. Closing the first book, she picked up another. "This was taken on his first day of kindergarten," she said, pointing. "Sam took the picture. I don't know who cried more."

Jesse dipped his head over the book. "He doesn't look to me like he's crying. In fact, if he'd smiled much bigger, his face would have split wide open."

Mandy laughed, pressing her shoulder against his in the easy way a friend would when sharing a private joke. "I didn't mean him. I meant Sam and me."

Still smiling, Mandy turned another page while Jesse turned his gaze on her. "They've been an important part of his life, haven't they?"

Mandy turned to look at him. "You mean Sam and Merideth?"

Jesse nodded.

"Very much so. I'm afraid between us, we've spoiled him rotten."

Resentful of the wisp of hair that shadowed her face when she turned her gaze back to the album, Jesse lifted it and tucked it behind her ear, leaving his fingers to curve at the feminine shell. "He doesn't seem to have suffered any. He's a good kid. You've obviously done a good job raising him."

Mandy felt her cheeks warm and wasn't sure whether it was Jesse's touch or his compliment that drew the heat to them. But she knew she couldn't look at him. Not now, when her emotions were so close to the surface. "Thank you. I've done my best."

"At what price?"

Mandy jerked her head around to stare at him. "What do you mean?"

"Lucas couldn't have been happy about your having my son."

Mandy dropped her chin, unable to meet the sympathy in Jesse's gaze. "No, he wasn't. But it didn't matter. Not to me. I wanted Jaime, and no one was going to take him away from me. Not even my father.''

"You mean he tried?"

Mandy's shoulders sagged with the weight of the painful memories. "Not physically, though he did try to persuade me to have an abortion or at the least put Jaime up for adoption.''

"But you didn't.''

Mandy shook her head, still unable to look at Jesse. If she did, she was afraid that he'd see the truth in her eyes—the fact that she'd defied her father because she wanted so desperately to keep a part of Jesse with her always. "No. And I've never regretted my decision.''

"Thank you.''

Surprised, Mandy turned to look at him again. Unshed tears glimmered in the soft lamplight. "For what?''

"For standing up to Lucas *and* for giving me Jaime.''

Mandy simply stared, robbed of a reply by the hand that slipped from her ear and down her back to settle at her waist, drawing her closer. She shivered, unblinking, unable to look away.

"I should never have left,'' he said, his voice husky.

"Why did you?'' she whispered.

Jesse stiffened, reminded of that night long ago. "You made your choice. Remember? You chose Lucas over me.''

Mandy's mouth dropped open. "No,'' she cried, shaking her head in denial. "I didn't.''

Jesse's forehead pleated into a frown. "Then why didn't you leave with me?''

Mandy turned, angling her body toward him, and the album slipped from her knees and fell to the carpet forgotten. "If I'd left with you, Lucas would've been furious. He would never have let you leave that glen alive. I was just trying to buy us time until we could figure out a way to be together."

Jesse let his head drop back and groaned. "But I thought—"

Mandy pressed a finger to his lips, drawing his face back down to hers. "No, Jesse. The only thing I ever wanted was to be with you."

He caught her hand in his and squeezed. "Oh, Mandy. If only I hadn't let my pride get in the way. I could've been here for you and Jaime."

She smiled softly. "You're here for him now."

Jesse sighed, taking her hand to his heart. "Yes. And I'm here for you, too."

Mandy felt the thud of his heartbeat and her own pulse quickened in response. "Jesse?"

"Yes?"

"Why did you leave me in the barn last night without saying goodbye?"

Jesse closed his eyes, and blew out a long breath, caught off guard by the question. When he opened them again, Mandy was still looking at him, her green eyes filled with expectancy. "I don't know," he said miserably. "Scared, I guess."

"Of me?"

Jesse snorted. "No. Of me. Of what you made me feel."

"What did you feel?"

The intensity of her gaze trapped Jesse and he realized there was no escape. "It was like nothing had changed, no time had passed since the last time I held you."

"But there was a change, Jesse. You never made

love to me like you did last night. It was as if you were trying to punish me for something."

That she could so accurately name his original intent shook Jesse to the bone. "I'm sorry. I didn't mean to hurt you."

She leaned closer, wanting to reassure him. "You didn't. Not physically, anyway."

The scent he'd smelled earlier grew stronger until his brain grew fuzzy and his senses heightened, blinding him to all but the woman whose hand still rested on his heart. "Mandy," he murmured, his voice growing husky. "Oh, Mandy," he sighed as he dipped his face to claim her lips.

With the first brush of his mouth against hers, Mandy felt the difference. Softness, tenderness, regret. Nothing at all like that first kiss the night before when his lips had punished, his hands had demanded retribution for a crime she was innocent of.

This was Jesse. Her Jesse. The man she'd fallen in love with as a teenaged girl. Tearing her hand from his, she threw her arms around his neck and clung. He responded with a groan that rose from deep in his throat and climbed to vibrate against her lips like a guitar's plucked string. Twisting around, he used his chest to ease her to the bed and Mandy went willingly, holding his face to hers with fingers twined in his thick black hair. She wouldn't, couldn't let go of him. Not now, not when they'd finally put to rest that night from long ago when they'd each thought they'd lost the other. Not ever.

His hand slipped inside her robe and Mandy gasped, arching to meet him, then grew limp, her shoulders sinking back to the tangled sheets as he palmed a bare breast. Closing her eyes, she gave herself up to each stroke of his fingers, each scrape of his thumb across her sensitized nipple. The gentleness, the utter tenderness of his touch, drew memories of other times he'd touched her just so. Now, as she had then, she quickly grew impatient to touch him as well.

She skimmed her hands across the breadth of his back, feeling each corded muscle, each swell and dip of his spine. When her fingers inadvertently brushed against the bandage she'd placed there, he flinched and she immediately stilled. "I'm sorry. I didn't mean to hurt you."

He lifted his head to look at her, his eyes dark with a passion that fevered her skin. "It's just a little tender is all. You didn't hurt me."

Smiling softly, she smoothed her hands upwards, over the sharp blades of his shoulders, to frame his face with her hands. "I love you, Jesse," she whispered. "I've never stopped loving you."

The truth of it was there in her eyes, in the soft curve of her lips. *"Querida,"* he groaned, reverting to his native language. "My love." He shifted, dipping his head, and took her mouth with his as he shucked out of his jeans. With his tongue, he prepared her, teased her with what was to come.

Once free of his jeans, he braced his hands on the mattress on either side of her head and lowered himself to her. Lifting his head, he met her gaze, watching as the passion built on her face. With a tenderness that brought tears to her eyes, he entered her, then carried her higher with each slow, measured thrust until she was gasping beneath him. He increased the rhythm, carrying them both higher and higher, until perspiration beaded their skins like early-morning dew.

He felt the explosion build within her, felt her nails

dig into his back, and knew she was near the edge. Cupping his hands beneath her hips, he brought her hard against him, thrusting one last time…and felt her shatter around him. Then and only then did he allow himself the release that he so desperately needed.

Weakened by spent passion, he gathered her into his arms and pulled her on top of him. Her robe tangled around his legs and a pain shot through his back as he took her full weight. But Jesse didn't care. Mandy loved him and that was all that mattered. Wrapping his arms around her, he drew her head to his shoulder.

"Sleep, *querida*. Sleep," he murmured.

Dawn brought sunlight to the room, but no regrets for Mandy. She'd awakened him every hour through the night, fearing he'd suffered a concussion from Judas' attack. As a result, neither of them had gotten much sleep.

The lump on his head had decreased somewhat in size during the night, but was already beginning to turn a vibrant shade of purple. Tenderly she placed her lips there, feeling more than a bit responsible for him being hurt.

"What was that for?"

Mandy smiled at the grogginess in his voice. "Just a little kiss for medicinal purposes."

Yawning, Jesse hooked an arm around her waist and snugged her closer. "Medicinal, huh?" he murmured, closing his eyes again.

Enjoying this early-morning pillow talk, Mandy inched closer. "Does it feel better?"

"'It' being the knot on my head?"

"Yes," she replied, chuckling. "What else did you think I meant?"

"Well, you could've been asking about my back."

Mandy lifted her head, instantly concerned. "Does your back hurt?"

"No, but there is something else that's beginning to ache a little."

Hearing the teasing in his voice, Mandy gave his chest a hard shove. "You jerk!"

Jesse chuckled, catching her hand in his. "Had you worried there for a minute, didn't I?"

Huffily, Mandy settled her cheek back on her hand. "Only for a minute."

"Let's get married."

Mandy's head immediately popped right back up. "What did you say?"

Jesse wasn't sure when the idea had occurred to him, nor was he sure why he'd blurted out the suggestion so bluntly, but he never questioned the rightness of it. They were destined for each other, had been since the day they'd first met. But Mandy's shock had him propping himself up on one elbow to meet her gaze. "I said let's get married."

Slowly, Mandy pushed herself to a sitting position, scraping her hair back from her face with two hands. "Married?" she repeated dully as she stared at the far wall.

"Yeah, married. You know, 'I do,' 'you do,' husband and wife."

Mandy hauled in a shuddery breath before turning to look at him. "Jesse, we can't."

"We can't?" he repeated in disbelief. "But you said you loved me, and I love you. Isn't that all that's required for a man and woman to decide to spend their lives together?"

Seeing that she'd hurt him, Mandy laid a hand on his cheek. "Yes, but...but what about Jaime?"

"What about him? He's my son and it's past time I claimed him as such."

Twisting around to face him, Mandy tried her best to explain. "But, Jesse, as far as Jaime is concerned, you and I have only known each other for just a few weeks. To suddenly announce that we're getting married, then to drop the bomb on him that you're his father..." She shook her head, pressing her palms against her temples as she envisioned what a shock that would be for her son. "We just can't," she repeated. "It's simply too soon."

"For who? You or Jaime?"

Mandy dropped her hands, surprised by the bitterness in his voice. "For Jaime," she said, touching a hand to his cheek. "It's Jaime I'm concerned about. We've got to consider his feelings in all this."

Though she could tell Jesse wasn't happy with her decision, she could feel the tension ease from his face.

"Okay. But we're not dragging this out forever," he warned her. "We've wasted enough time as it is."

"He didn't come home last night, did he?"

Pete heaved a block of salt lick into the back of his truck. "Wouldn't know," he replied as he dusted coarse granules from his hands. "I don't keep track of the boy's whereabouts like you do."

Margo thinned her lips. "But you'd know if he came home or not. You *do* share the bunkhouse with him."

"Yep, as a matter of fact I do." Pete tipped back his hat and grinned which had Margo's lips thinning even more. "But I sleep like the dead. Once I'm out,

a herd of spooked buffalo could stampede right through
the bunkhouse and I'd never be the wiser.''

''I suppose you think that's funny,'' Margo snapped.

''No, ma'am. As a matter of fact, I don't.'' He
stooped to pick up another block of salt lick and hefted
it to his shoulder, then turned to grin at her again. ''But
I do find it amusin' that you're concerned about where
and how Jesse spends his time. Might make another
man wonder if you weren't worried just a bit about the
boy's safety.'' He heaved the salt onto the back of the
truck and chuckled as he turned to her again. ''But of
course we both know that's not true, now don't we,
Margo?''

Later that same morning, Mandy turned to glance
out her office window when she heard a truck on the
drive beyond. A black semi pulling a long, custom-
built horse trailer passed by on the way to the barn.
Pushing out of her chair, she pressed her nose to the
window to read the writing on the side of the trailer.

Barrister Farms. Noble, Oklahoma.

''What in the world?'' she murmured under her
breath. Tossing her pen aside, she ran for the door and
through the house, anxious to find out what the truck
was doing on the Double-Cross.

At the barn, she stopped, breathless, to find Jesse
standing behind the trailer talking to the truck's driver
as he unhooked the trailer's rear door and swung it
wide.

''Jesse?''

He turned to look at her and a smile broadened on
his face. Mandy felt the heat of it all the way to her
toes. ''Good morning,'' he said, his voice husky.

''Good morning to you, too,'' she replied as she

stepped closer. She waved her hand at the trailer. "What is all this?"

A blush stained Jesse's cheeks. "A little surprise for Jaime. I hope you don't mind?"

Mandy let out a nervous breath. "Before I tell you if I mind or not, maybe you should tell me what the surprise is."

Jesse cut a glance at the man who stood beside him. "Mandy, I'd like you to meet the foreman of my ranch in Oklahoma, Jim Bonner. Jim, this is Mandy Mc-Cloud."

The man scraped off his hat and extended his hand. "Pleased to meet you, ma'am."

Surprised to learn that Jesse had a ranch in Oklahoma, Mandy shook the foreman's hand. "I'm pleased to meet you, too, Mr. Bonner." As soon as he released her hand, she turned to Jesse again. "Do you mind telling me what is going on here?"

Jesse chuckled. "Well, since Jaime's pretty much mastered roping that bale of hay, I thought he might need a roping horse to test his skills on, so I had one of mine shipped down here." He stepped to the side, gesturing toward the back of the trailer. "Want a look?"

Unable to resist, Mandy stepped to the back of the trailer and peered inside. The interior was state-of-the-art; stainless-steel railings topped with black padding. From the center slant, a paint horse turned his head to stare at her. "Oh, my goodness," she murmured. "He's beautiful."

"He's that, all right, and a damned good roping horse to boot."

"Do you raise horses on your ranch in Oklahoma?"

Jesse nodded. "And train them, too. This paint was

one of my first foals.'' Anxious to unload the horse,
Jesse dropped the ramp, unhooked the chain and
climbed inside the trailer. Murmuring softly to the animal, he unhooked the lead rope and backed the horse
down the ramp, still clucking to him.

Mandy stepped back, giving the horse room, then
joined Jesse at the paint's head. ''Oh, he's gorgeous,''
she said, stroking his velvet muzzle. ''Does Jaime
know about this?''

''No. I wanted to surprise him.''

Mandy turned to look at him. ''Oh, he'll be surprised
all right,'' she replied dryly. ''I'll be lucky if he does
another chore for the rest of the summer.''

''We could put some restrictions on him,'' Jesse offered, lifting a hand to scratch the horse between his
ears.

At the word ''we,'' Mandy felt her heart flutter. The
idea of sharing parental responsibilities didn't bother
her in the least, and that Jesse was willing to share the
burden pleased her immensely. ''Such as?'' she
prompted, anxious to hear what he had to say.

''Well, how about if we tell him he can't ride until
he has all his chores done?''

''And if he breaks the rules?''

Jesse chuckled. ''Then he faces the consequences.''

Intrigued by the ease with which Jesse had stepped
into the role of father, she turned to look up at him
curiously. ''What would be the consequences?''

Jesse dipped his head, scratching at his chin. ''I suppose we'd have to deprive him of something that brings
him the most pleasure, just to make our point. Seems
to me, that would be to deny him the privilege of riding
for a day or two.'' Inexperienced with dealing with

kids and discipline, Jesse lifted his gaze to Mandy's, seeking her approval. "Would that be appropriate?"

Mandy smiled. "Perfectly. But I think it would also be appropriate for *you* to explain the consequences to him *and* enforce them, since you're the one who's giving him the horse."

"Coward," Jesse teased.

Mandy looked up at him and grinned. "Maybe, but I play the villain often enough in his life. I think it's time you became someone more than just his friend."

"Hey! Whose horse is that?"

Mandy and Jesse both turned to find Jaime racing across the barnyard toward them. Biting back a smile, Mandy folded her arms beneath her breasts. "No time like the present," she murmured, just loud enough for Jesse to hear.

Margo dropped the phone back onto its base, cursing violently, then immediately picked it up again and punched in a series of numbers. "Representative Gaines, please. Margo Barrister calling."

She waited only a few seconds before the legislator's booming voice came over the wire. "Margo, how are you?"

"Fine, Matthew. And you?"

"Better now that I'm talking to you," he teased. "What can I do for you?"

Margo caught the phone cord between her fingers and spun her chair to stare out Wade's office window— her office now, she was quick to remind herself. "I was wondering if you got that check I mailed for your campaign fund?"

"Yes, I did. And a generous one, I might add. Thank you."

"No thanks needed, Matthew. I always consider my contributions to your campaign an investment." She tipped forward in her chair, watching as Jesse's truck raced by on its way to the bunkhouse. "I need a small favor, Matthew," she murmured, narrowing an eye at Jesse as he swung down from the truck's cab.

"As always, Margo, I'm at your service, both as the representative from your district and as a dear friend."

Margo frowned at the sugarcoated reply. She hated politicians, but then again, she had found her association with them had paid off for her now and again over the years. "I've just heard a rumor that someone is going to make an offer on the Circle Bar."

Matthew's voice took a sympathetic turn. "I'm so sorry, Margo. I'd heard that Wade didn't leave the ranch to you."

Margo had to fight back the urge to scream. To think that her private affairs were being bandied about the capital like common gossip sickened her as much as had hearing the terms of Wade's will read to her. Tightening her fingers on the receiver, she replied carefully, "Thank you for your concern, Matthew." Then, forcing a laugh, she added, "But what in the world would I want with the ranch? I find it difficult enough to find the time to manage my own investments." She took a steadying breath. "But it is my concern for the ranch that spawned this call.

"You know how much Wade wanted the ranch to stay in the family," she explained. "That's why he left it to Jesse." She shuddered at the sour taste the bastard's name left in her mouth.

"So what's the problem?" Matthew quizzed.

"Well," Margo replied, taking on a secretive tone. "Jesse has indicated that he wants to sell out."

"Oh, that's too bad. I'm sure Wade would be disappointed if he knew that."

"Yes, he would. But the worst part is that I'm afraid it is the McClouds who are wanting to purchase the Circle Bar. Wade would never want the Circle Bar to fall into the hands of the McClouds. And that's why I'm calling you. A source who must remain unnamed has just told me that Amanda McCloud has set up a dummy corporation to make the purchase, hoping that no one will discover her part in the exchange until the deed has been transferred."

"And?" Matthew prodded.

"I want you to find out if that information is true. Can you make a few calls? Perhaps talk to the Secretary of State to check to see what letters of incorporation have been filed and who the directors are?"

"Of course, Margo. Anything for you."

A satisfied smile curved at Margo's lips. "Thank you, Matthew. I knew I could count on you."

Jesse barreled into the bunkhouse, grabbed his duffle bag and dumped its contents onto his cot.

Pete glanced up from his easy chair where he was reading the paper. "Goin' somewhere?" he asked dryly.

Jesse stuffed a pair of jeans and a clean shirt back into the bag. "Yeah. I'm taking Jaime and Mandy on a camp-out." He turned, scraping his shaving gear and comb from the shelf above the sink, and added it to the bag.

Pete rested the paper on his knees. "A campin' trip, huh? Sounds like the three of you are gettin' purdy cozy."

A smile spread across Jesse's face as he cocked his

head to look at his old friend. "Yeah, you could say that."

Pete nodded his approval, then frowned. "Margo came lookin' for you this mornin'. Wanted to know if you'd come in last night."

Jesse paused, a rolled pair of socks in his hand. "What did you tell her?"

Pete snorted and picked up his paper again, giving it a snap before disappearing behind its pages. "That I sleep like the dead and wouldn't know if a herd of buffalo had stampeded by my bed."

Jesse chuckled and gave Pete's boot a kick with his own. "Well, at least you didn't have to lie. You *do* sleep like the dead."

Pete grunted. "That's what *you* think." He lowered the paper and grinned slyly at Jesse over its top. "Where *did* you sleep last night, anyways?"

Embarrassed, Jesse looked away, though he had to hide a smile of his own. He stuffed the socks into the duffle bag and zipped it closed. "Let's just say I didn't sleep alone."

Pete's grin quickly turned into a frown again as he leaned forward to squint at Jesse. "What happened to your head?"

Jesse lifted a hand to touch at the scrape on his temple. With all that had happened in between, he'd totally forgotten about his run-in with Judas. "Had a fight with a stallion."

"And you lost?"

Jesse's smile was easy and quick...and just a touch sheepish. "The first round. But the battle's not over yet."

"Did you get throwed?"

"No. Kicked."

"Kicked!" Pete sat up straighter, his eyebrows shooting up. "I thought I learned you better than that. 'Always stay clear of a horse's hind end.' Ain't that what I taught you?"

"Yes, sir, you did. But he jerked me down and turned on me before I had a chance to get out of the way."

Pete gave his paper another snap and lifted it in front of his face again. "I guess I'll have to go over there and bust that horse out myself 'fore you get yourself killed."

Jesse hooked the strap of his duffle bag over his shoulder as a wad of emotion rose to his throat. Pete might be gruff, but Jesse knew that what the old man was saying was that he cared. And there were few people in Jesse's life who had ever cared about him. Pete. His mother. Mandy.

On the way to the door, he stopped and put a hand on Pete's arm. "Thanks, Pete."

Pete's Adam's apple bobbed and he quickly shucked off Jesse's hand. "Get on out of here," he grumped, "'fore I decide to tell Margo your plans."

Seven

Thirty minutes later, whistling happily, Jesse snagged his duffle bag from the back of his truck and headed for the barn where he was to meet Mandy and Jaime for their camping trip. About halfway there, he stopped, his attention caught by the sound of a man's voice, raised in anger, coming from inside the barn.

"You stupid wetback! What'n the hell do you think you're doin'?"

At the word "wetback" Jesse's blood turned to ice. He'd been called that and worse through the years, and even though the racial slur hadn't been hurled at him personally, hearing it drew the same results. His lips curled in anger and his fingers tightened on the straps of his duffle bag.

"Nothin', I swear," came a small voice.

Jaime? The fear in the boy's voice had Jesse running

the remaining distance to the barn. Once inside, he tossed the duffle bag to the ground.

"What's going on here?" he demanded angrily of the wrangler who had Jaime pinned to the barn wall.

The cowboy didn't even spare Jesse a glance. "Mind your own damn bizness," he muttered, tightening his hand on the front of Jaime's shirt and hauling him higher up the wall. "I told you to stay away from my stuff, now didn't I?" he raged on. "Didn't I?" he repeated, raising his voice an octave higher when Jaime didn't immediately answer.

Jaime swallowed hard. "Yessir."

"Well, now you're gonna pay." The wrangler released Jaime and reached for the buckle on his belt. Whipping the thick strap of leather from his belt loops, he quickly folded it in half and gave it a spine-chilling snap. He had the belt raised head high when Jesse's hand caught the strap and brought it down, using it to jerk the cowboy's hand behind his back.

The cowboy reeled, eyes blazing. "I told you to mind your own bizness," he said through clenched teeth.

Though Jesse wanted to tell the man to get his filthy hands off his son, he couldn't. Instead he said, "Jaime *is* my business."

Using the one hand still free, the cowboy fisted it and took a swing at Jesse. But Jesse was quicker and stronger. He caught the man's hand before it hit its mark and had the guy up against the wall, his hands pinned above his head.

"I mighta knowed," the cowboy spat out. "You wetbacks always stick together."

Rage, red-hot and numbing, blinded Jesse to all but the face of the man in front of him. Dropping a hand, he clenched his fist and buried it in the man's stomach. Once. Twice. Three times. The cowboy managed one pitiful moan before he bent double, sucking at air.

"Jesse! My God! What are you doing?"

Mandy's voice came from behind him. She grabbed for his arm, but Jesse shrugged it off, delivering another blow, this time to the cowboy's face. The punch caught the man under the chin and sent him slamming back against the wall. Blood oozed from the corner of his mouth, while his eyes rolled back in his head.

Horrified, Mandy fought her way between the two men, pressing her hands against Jesse's chest. "Stop it!" she cried. "Stop it right now!"

In disgust, Jesse dropped the hand that had kept the cowboy upright, and Mandy had to leap out of the way when he slid to the barn floor, groaning.

She planted her hands on her hips as she whirled to face Jesse. "What in the world is going on here?" she demanded angrily.

Jesse stooped to scrape his hat off the ground. "He called Jaime a wetback," he growled. "He was going to whip him."

Mandy's eyebrows shot up and her mouth dropped open.

"Whip him!" She spun to stare at Jaime. "Oh, baby," she cried, rushing to gather him in her arms. Then she quickly pushed him to arm's length so that she could see him. "Did he hurt you?"

Jaime, still pale and shaking, managed a wobbly smile. "Nah. Jesse had him up against the wall and was beating the tar out of him before he had the chance."

Dropping her arms from her son, she spun again, but this time to glare down at her wrangler. "You're fired," she said tersely. "Pack your gear and get out. And don't you *ever* dare show your face on the Double-Cross again. Do you understand me?"

The cowboy pushed to his feet, his eyes glinting with a meanness that would rival that found in the eyes of the devil himself. "Loud and clear." He scraped the back of his hand across his mouth, smearing the blood across his cheek. "I never liked workin' for no bitchin' woman, anyhow."

The three horses plodded slowly across the pasture and started a slow climb up a short hill. Mandy and Jesse, riding with their son between them, were still caught in a pensive silence, a result of the ugly scene in the barn.

Jaime didn't seem to share their somber mood.

"You were terrific, Jesse!" Jaime doubled his hand into a fist and hit the air three times. "Bam! Bam! Bam!" He tossed back his head and laughed. "And did you see Rube's face? He didn't stand a chance. Boy, wait 'til I tell Davie."

Though he heard the pride in his son's voice, Jesse was ashamed that Jaime had witnessed the violent attack. "Fighting is wrong, Jaime. A man should always keep his temper in check."

Jaime twisted in his saddle to look at Jesse in surprise. "But he had it coming! He called me a wetback, and he called you one, too!"

Jesse and Mandy exchanged a look over their son's head. Mandy's face showed concern; Jesse's, regret. "That's just a word, son, and words can't hurt us. You have to learn to let them roll off of you like water on a duck's back."

Jaime's face fell. "But don't it make you mad when somebody calls you names?"

"Doesn't it," Mandy corrected without thinking.

Jaime frowned at her over his shoulder before turning back to Jesse. "*Doesn't* it make you mad?"

Jesse let out a sigh. "Yeah, it does. But it doesn't give me the right to hit anyone. Fighting just lowers me to their level. Some people are prejudiced—thank God not everyone—and can't see past the color of a person's skin, or his nationality. But that's their problem, not ours."

Jaime kept his gaze on Jesse, his forehead creased in puzzlement. "Then what do you do when people call you names?"

"Ignore them. I've learned the hard way that in doing so, I rob them of their power over me." Hoping to change the subject to a lighter one, he asked, "Did you remember to pack your fishing rod?"

Jaime reached behind him and patted his bedroll. "Right here. Think we'll catch us any fish?"

Jesse grinned, then leaned over to ruffle his son's hair. "I hope so. If not, we're all going to bed hungry."

Jesse sat with his back propped against the trunk of a tree, his fishing rod balanced between his knees. Mandy lay stretched out on a blanket to his left, sunning, while Jaime fished a narrow channel at the far end of the lake.

"I'm sorry."

Mandy lifted her head to peer at Jesse. "For what?"

Jesse dipped his head and picked up a small stone from the ground. "For what happened in the barn."

Mandy pushed herself to a sitting position, anxious

to reassure him. "You were only trying to protect Jaime."

Jesse lifted the stone and hurled it, watching it skip across the water. "Yes, but I should have sent him to the house before dealing with Rube. Jaime didn't need to witness that kind of violence."

"He's seen fistfights before."

Jesse glanced her way, his forehead creased by a frown.

Mandy lifted a shoulder, then got to her feet. Crossing to him, she sat down beside him. "You know how short tempers can get when a bunch of men are working together on a ranch. More often than not, disagreements end in a fight."

Jesse's frown deepened as he shifted his gaze to stare at the lake. "Yeah, but he hasn't seen me fighting."

Mandy placed a hand on his thigh and squeezed. "Don't be so hard on yourself. Jaime's even been in a few fights himself."

Jesse turned to look at her. "He has?"

Mandy nodded. "Though I certainly don't approve. And several of the fights started exactly as the one today in the barn, with name-calling."

"He's been called a wetback before?"

"And spic, beaner, greaser, foreign-exchange student." She waved a hand as if to lessen the words' importance. "Nothing that you haven't heard before."

Sighing, Jesse gathered her hand in his, lacing his fingers with hers. "I'd hoped it would be easier for Jaime, him being a McCloud, and all."

"Having the McCloud name behind him doesn't change the fact that he is part-Mexican."

Jesse glanced up, his gaze meeting hers and holding.

"No," he replied slowly. "The same as Barrister never made being part-Mexican any easier for me."

From his spot downstream, Jaime glanced back over his shoulder and saw that his mother had moved from her blanket and was sitting by Jesse. And Jesse was even holding her hand!

Jaime did a high-five at the sky, danced an end-zone jive that would have made Deion Sanders jealous...and very nearly fell in the lake. Catching himself just short of falling, he grinned, remembering the number of times Jesse had called him "son."

Son! Jaime thought in wonder and decided he liked the sound of the word when it came from Jesse. He'd always wanted a dad, though he'd hidden the fact from his mother, thinking it would make her feel bad.

"Mama and Jesse," he whispered in awe. "Man, it can't get any better than this!"

"Mama, tell the story of how the Double-Cross got its name again."

Mandy smiled at her son over the campfire. Though Jaime had heard the story a million times, he never tired of hearing it told again.

"Well," she began. "Back in the mid-1800s two friends decided to pool their money and buy a five-thousand-acre tract of land in the Texas hill country. Their names were—"

"Bart McCloud and Blade Barrister," Jaime interjected quickly.

Mandy laughed. "Yes. Those were their names. And they named their ranch the Circle Bar."

Jaime turned to Jesse and explained for his benefit, "The Barristers kept the Circle Bar name when the ranches divided, but the McClouds named theirs the Double-Cross Heart.''

Jesse bit back a smile. He knew the story well, but he decided to humor his son. "Is that a fact?''

"Yep, it is.'' Jaime turned back to Mandy, motioning for her to go on. "Hurry up, Mama, tell the story.''

Mandy arched a brow. "Are you sure you don't want to tell it?''

Jaime wagged his head. "No, you tell it better. But get to the good part where they have the big fight.''

Mandy resumed the tale. "While in Kansas City selling a herd of cattle, Bart fell in love with a beautiful young woman whose name was—''

"Amanda Grayson,'' Jaime interrupted again. He turned to Jesse, smiling proudly. "Mama's named after her. My grandmother thought it was romantic-soundin'.''

Mandy pursed her lips and frowned at her son. "Are you sure you don't want to tell the story?''

Jaime grinned sheepishly. "Nah. I promise I'll be quiet.''

"Well—'' Mandy eyed her son dubiously for a moment, then caught up the thread of the story again. "Bart married Amanda and brought her home with him to Texas to live on the Circle Bar. Since he and Blade shared a house, Amanda lived there, too.

"One day Bart was out working cattle and returned home unexpectedly and found Blade and Amanda in a compromising position.''

Jaime chuckled, elbowing Jesse in the ribs. "He caught 'em doin' the wild thing.''

Jesse sputtered a laugh, then quickly covered it when he saw Mandy's frown.

"As I was saying,'' Mandy went on pointedly, turning her frown on her son. "Bart caught them together and he was so mad and so hurt by his wife's infidelity that he left and never went back. He set up camp on the far side of the ranch and sent word to Blade that he wanted to divide their ranch in two. Bart took the twenty-five hundred acres to the north and left Blade the twenty-five hundred acres to the south."

"And was Amanda happy with Blade?" Jaime prodded eagerly.

"No," Mandy replied, smiling sadly. "She regretted her mistake until the day she died. You see, Blade was a mean-spirited man. He didn't truly love Amanda the way Bart did. He just wanted her because Bart had her, and he couldn't stand Bart to have something that he didn't. Once he had Amanda, Blade didn't want her anymore. Realizing the foolishness of her mistake, Amanda went to Bart and tried to persuade him to forgive her, but Bart wouldn't. She'd broken his heart."

Mandy shook her head, as if clearing the memory. "Anyway, Bart never got over the loss of Amanda, or the fact that Blade had betrayed his trust. So he named his ranch the Double-Cross Heart, as a constant reminder to Blade and everyone else in the community of Blade's betrayal."

Jaime turned to Jesse. "And that's why the Barristers and the McClouds have feuded all these years," he finished proudly. "And the Barristers to this day are all still a bunch of dirty, stinking liars and thieves to boot."

As soon as the words were out of his mouth, Jaime's chin sagged and his face reddened. "Gosh, Jesse. I'm sorry. I forget that you're a Barrister."

Jesse dropped back his head and laughed. He shifted his plate to his knee so that he could reach over and give Jaime's shoulder a playful slug. "Don't worry, kid, there have been times when I've called them the same thing."

"Eat your dinner, Jaime," Mandy ordered. "I think that's enough storytelling for one night."

Seeing that Mandy was as mortified by Jaime's statement as the boy was, Jesse sought to lighten the mood. "Mmm-mmm," he said with feeling as he set his plate aside. "That was the best fried catfish I've ever eaten. And these hush puppies." He popped the last one in his mouth and closed his eyes on a sigh. "They melt in your mouth."

Jaime tucked his tongue to the corner of his mouth and nabbed a blob of ketchup, then grinned. "My mama's the best cook in the whole wide world. And she's pretty, too, isn't she?"

Jesse glanced up to smile at Mandy over the campfire. "Yes, she surely is."

"Oh, stop it, you two," Mandy fussed, embarrassed by the praise. "I already said I'd clean up the dishes, so you don't have to bribe me with compliments."

"I'll clean up," Jaime quickly offered, jumping to his feet to grab his mother's plate. "Why don't you two take a walk before it gets too dark to see?"

Mandy and Jesse shared a surprised look. "All right," Jesse said slowly. He held out a hand. "Mandy?"

With a bewildered glance at her son, Mandy stepped around the campfire, accepting Jesse's hand. "Be careful with the fire," she warned Jaime.

"I will. Y'all just enjoy the moonlight. Oh, and don't be in any rush to get back," he added. "I think I'll go on to bed once I'm finished with the dishes."

"'Enjoy the moonlight'?" Mandy whispered as

Jesse guided her down the path to the lake. "And what in the world did he mean by 'don't be in any rush to get back'?"

Jesse dropped her hand to sling an arm around her shoulders and draw her close as they walked down the path side-by-side. "I think our son is trying his hand at a little matchmaking."

Mandy stopped so fast, she had Jesse stumbling. "Matchmaking!" she cried. "You mean—"

Jesse turned, chuckling, to gather her into his arms. "Yes, that's exactly what I mean." He dipped his head over hers and dropped a quick kiss on her lips.

Her eyes round in wonder, Mandy continued to stare up at him. "He's never— But then I've never—" She pressed her forehead to Jesse's chin and groaned. "I didn't even know he thought about stuff like this."

Jesse's chuckle rumbled beneath her hand. "You probably don't want to know what thoughts he has. I remember at his age, I was—"

Mandy leaned back to clap a hand over Jesse's mouth. "No, please," she begged him. "Don't say it. I'd rather think of my son as an innocent little boy a while longer."

Taking her hand from his mouth, Jesse chuckled and laced his fingers through hers again as he continued on to the lake. "He can't remain your little boy forever, you know."

Mandy sighed, stopping at the lake's edge to turn to him. Unexpected tears misted her eyes. "I know. But I can't bear the thought of him growing up and leaving me some day."

"Have you ever considered having more children?"

"I wanted to, but..." The explanation drifted away unfinished.

"But what?"

Though it took courage to do so, Mandy met his gaze squarely. "You were the only man I ever wanted to have children with and you left."

"I'm here now," he offered softly.

A slow smile grew on Mandy's face at the hope and sincerity she saw in his eyes. "Jaime's always wanted a little brother or sister."

Jesse pulled her hips more firmly against his. "Why don't we see what we can do about giving him one?"

Margo pulled up beside the gasoline pump and lowered her window, glancing nervously about. Just as she was about to give up and drive away, Rube stepped out of the shadows of the building. She frowned as he approached her car.

"What do you mean calling me at this hour of the night?" she demanded angrily. "And I told you *never* to leave a message with my housekeeper! I don't want anyone to know of our association."

Rube stuck his head in the open window and rested his elbows on the window brace. "Well, now that's just too bad, Miss High-and-Mighty Lady."

Margo smelled the liquor immediately and drew back sharply. "You've been drinking," she said in distaste.

"A man's got a right to take a sip now and again."

Margo put one hand on the wheel and the other on the gearshift. "Contact me when you're sober. I refuse to talk to you when you're drunk."

Rube's hand shot out and covered hers on the wheel. Margo snapped her head around to glare at him.

"I wouldn't be in such an all-fired hurry if I were you," he said in a low voice.

Margo heard the threat and tried to twist free, regretting her impulsiveness in responding to his late-night call. But his grip remained firm. She lifted her chin imperiously. "If you have information for me, then say so. I need to get back to the ranch before someone discovers I'm gone."

Rube's hold on her hand softened to a caress. "Oh, I have information, all right, but it's gonna cost you."

Margo tried her best to hide her revulsion. "How much?"

"Twice what you gave me before."

She jerked her hand from his and opened her purse. She quickly pulled the bills from her wallet and thrust them at him.

He took the money and fanned it once beneath his nose before stuffing it in his pocket. "I jist love the smell of money, don't you?"

"The information," Margo reminded him tersely. "What have you got?"

"Right now Jesse, the boy and that McCloud bitch are all out on a camp-out. They took their horses and were plannin' on gettin' in a little fishin' before makin' camp out by Double-Cross Lake."

Margo narrowed her eyes, thinking. The setup was perfect to do away not only with Jesse, but the McCloud woman and her illegitimate son, as well. It wasn't all that uncommon to find campers murdered while they slept. She stole a glance at Rube, and immediately discarded the idea. She couldn't trust him to carry out such a scheme, especially not in the condition he was in. "When are they planning on returning?" she asked instead.

"Tomorrow 'bout noon."

"I want to know the second they return. Call my

house and let the phone ring once, then hang up. I'll know it's you."

"And how much are you gonna give me for spyin' for you this time?"

"We'll talk about that later. You just make sure you follow my instructions." Before he could respond, Margo jerked the car into gear and stomped on the accelerator. Rube stumbled back out of the way just shy of getting the toes of his boots run over.

"Bitch," he muttered under his breath. "You'll pay, all right. And it may be with more than money." He spat on the ground, then turned, weaving his way back into the shadows.

"Do you have to go now?"

Jesse heard the disappointment in Jaime's voice and had to bite back a grin. The fact that his son wanted him around pleased him enormously. "I've just got to check on a few things over at the Circle Bar. I won't be long."

"How long?"

Jesse chuckled and tossed his duffle bag into the back of his truck. "A couple of hours. Maybe longer." He climbed into the truck and closed the door, then stuck his head out the open window. "Depends on how much needs my attention."

Jaime sighed and stepped away from the truck as Jesse started the engine. "Well, hurry back," he called. "I want to try roping off my new horse."

Laughing, Jesse gave him a salute, and drove off. As he passed by the house, he slowed and gave his horn a short blast. Mandy appeared at her office window. He pressed two fingers to his lips and blew her a kiss.

Mandy did the same, then waved, smiling as Jesse drove on.

Margo had been up since five, pacing her office. By eight, she was on the phone. By ten, she was ready to tear her hair out. Surely someone must be privy to the McClouds' affairs! she told herself as she slammed the receiver back on its base.

While she was trying to think who to call next, her front doorbell rang. "I'll get it, Maria," she called as she headed for the front of the house. She swung the door wide to find a courier standing on her front porch.

"May I help you?"

"I have a delivery here for Jesse Barrister. Is he in?"

Margo pursed her lips in irritation. "No, he's out." As she started to close the door, she caught a glimpse of the return address on the large envelope the man held, and the name of Brickle & Stanton, Attorneys at Law. She quickly opened the door wide again, and became the model of southern hospitality. "But he should return at any minute," she offered helpfully. "If you'd like to leave the package, I'll personally see that he receives it."

Obviously relieved that he wouldn't have to make another trip to the boonies, the courier passed Margo a clipboard. "Just sign your name right here," he instructed, pointing.

With a flourish, Margo signed her name and passed the clipboard back. The courier, in turn, handed her the envelope. "Thank you, young man," she murmured graciously. "You can be assured that Jesse will receive the package the moment he returns."

As soon as she closed the front door, Margo hurried back to her office. Once inside, she closed the door and turned the envelope slowly, examining the closure. "Damn shipping tape," she muttered. "If they hadn't used that, I could've simply steamed it open, read the contents, then replaced them without Jesse ever being the wiser." She knew the tactic worked, because she'd read Wade's mail for years.

She sank down into her chair, tossing the envelope onto the desk in disgust. But as she sat there, staring at the offensive piece of mail, a thought occurred to her.

How would Jesse ever know who the package had been addressed to? Especially if she destroyed the envelope. Pulling open her lap drawer, she fished out a pair of scissors and snipped away at the tape. Holding her breath, she slid a legal document from the envelope. Skimming the first few pages, she realized that she was holding an offer to purchase the Circle Bar. Quickly flipping to the last page, she searched for the name of the intended purchaser.

JM Enterprises.

She grabbed for the phone and quickly punched in a series of numbers. "This is Margo Barrister. I need to speak with Representative Gaines immediately."

"I'm sorry, Mrs. Barrister, but he's in a meeting. May I take a message?"

"Tell him it's imperative that I speak to him this instant," Margo snapped impatiently.

She waited a moment while canned music chosen to soothe played monotonously in her ear.

"I'm so sorry to keep you waiting, Margo," the legislator soothed, oozing charm. "I had a constituent in my office. You know how tedious that can—"

"I have a name," Margo interrupted. "The corpo-

ration is under the name of JM Enterprises. Can you
trace it and find out if it is tied to the McClouds?''

"Certainly. I'll have an answer for you first thing in
the morning."

"I need an answer *now*," Margo demanded.

"Well, certainly. I'll call you back within the hour."
She slammed down the phone.

An hour, she thought, her nerves unraveling. What
if Jesse returned before she received the crucial information?

Picking up the shipping envelope the contract had
arrived in, she forced herself to calm down. It doesn't
matter what time he returns, she told herself. If he questions me on the time of the package's arrival, I'll simply lie and tell him it was only just delivered. Smiling,
she turned to the shredder on the credenza behind her
and fed the envelope through.

From the vantage point her living room offered of
the road leading to the Big House, Margo watched and
waited for Jesse's return. She sat in a Queen Anne chair
of crushed velvet, a magazine spread open across her
lap, unread.

The telephone rang and she started, thinking it might
be Matthew Gaines calling with the information she'd
requested. But before she could fully rise, the ringing
ceased. She waited, breathlessly, for a second ring.
When none was forthcoming, she sank back down,
curling her fingers around the chair's arms and smoothing her palms across the deep velvet. So he's back from
his little camp-out, she thought smugly. Thank you,
Rube, for the warning.

The telephone rang again and Margo rose, crossing
quickly to the entry table in the hallway to take the call

on the extension there. "Margo Barrister speaking," she said.

Gaines didn't waste any time. "You were right," he told her. "The corporation was set up by Mandy McCloud. Of course, her name is listed nowhere in the records, but I recognized the name of the McClouds' law firm and—"

"Brickle & Stanton," Margo interjected.

"Yes, Brickle and Stanton. I know one of the secretaries in the firm, so I gave her a call and found out that Mandy had the corporation set up several weeks ago for the sole purpose of purchasing the Circle Bar."

"Damn," Margo muttered bitterly.

"Is there anything more I can do?" Gaines asked helpfully.

Margo pursed her lips and thought a moment. "No," she finally said. "I can handle things from this point. But thank you, Matthew. You've been very helpful."

After replacing the phone, Margo crossed back to the living room and took her seat again, her gaze going straight to the window.

Now it was simply a matter of time. The Circle Bar would be hers, of that she was certain.

Jesse dumped his duffle bag on his bunk and had to fight the urge to follow it down. Yawning hugely, he stretched his arms high above his head, trying to get the kinks out of his back and shoulders. Groaning, he dropped his arms to press his hands against his lower back. If more camp-outs were going to be in his future, he was definitely going to invest in a more comfortable bedroll. He chuckled ruefully. Or maybe he should just swear off wild stallions.

A shower, he decided. That's what he needed to

loosen up his aching muscles. But before he could take one full step in that direction, the telephone rang. Quickly changing directions, he caught up the phone on the second ring. "Jesse Barrister," he said, identifying himself to the caller.

"Jesse, it's Margo, dear. If you have a moment, I'd like for you to come up to the Big House. There's a matter here that needs your attention."

Jesse bit back an oath. "Can it wait? I was just about to step into the shower."

"No. This is of the utmost importance."

Jesse sighed, looking longingly at the shower beyond the open bathroom door. "All right," he agreed reluctantly. "I'll be right there."

He dropped the phone and headed for the front door and his truck parked outside the bunkhouse. Within minutes, he was punching the front doorbell of the Big House. The door swung open, and Margo greeted him, dressed impeccably as always. Her expression gave no hint of the urgency she'd placed behind her request.

"Good morning, Jesse," she said in her silky southern drawl. She lifted her wrist, glancing at her wristwatch. "Or rather, good afternoon," she corrected pointedly.

"What do you want, Margo?"

She opened the door wider. "Please come inside, won't you? We'll be more comfortable discussing this matter in Wade's office."

Comfortable for whom? Jesse wondered. He'd never crossed the threshold of the Big House and didn't particularly want to now. Deciding that it might expedite things if he went along with Margo's request, he heaved a sigh and stepped inside. Margo closed the door behind him, gesturing for him to follow her.

"A package arrived earlier today by special courier," she explained as she entered the office and stepped behind the desk. She gathered the carefully folded document in her hands and extended it to Jesse. "Since you are the owner of the Circle Bar, you'll need to respond to this offer."

Jesse snapped his head up to meet her gaze. "Offer?"

"Yes," Margo confirmed. "Someone is interested in purchasing the Circle Bar."

Jesse took the papers from her and dropped down in a chair in front of the desk, eyeing her suspiciously. "You opened my mail?"

Margo lifted her chin. "I most certainly did. When something is delivered by special courier, it usually means it is important. Since you weren't here to take care of business," she added, her tone turning accusing, "I thought it in our best interest to check the contents of the envelope."

"*Our* best interest?" Jesse repeated.

"You may own the Circle Bar," she replied acidly. "But this is *my* home and what affects the Circle Bar affects me, as well. I, for one, intend to protect my interests."

Knowing that arguing with her was fruitless and would just delay his return to the Double-Cross, Jesse heaved a frustrated sigh and dipped his head over the document. He read quickly, skimming the pages, and emitted a low whistle when he saw the dollar amount offered in exchange for the deed to the Circle Bar. "Looks like more than a fair price," he murmured.

"Fair?" Margo repeated, obviously shocked by his reply. "That would depend on who was making the offer and the purpose behind it."

Jesse flipped several pages, skimming quickly. "JM Enterprises, Incorporated," he read. He glanced up to look at Margo who still stood behind the desk. "Never heard of them."

"You wouldn't have," she replied, her voice heavy with sarcasm. "It's a newly formed corporation."

Jesse dropped the papers to his knee in frustration. "You obviously know more about this than I do, so why don't you just share your knowledge with me and save us both some time."

"I have done a little research," Margo admitted carefully. "Just a few calls to determine the powers behind the corporation."

"And?" Jesse prodded, anxious to get this business over with and get back to the Double-Cross where Mandy and Jaime awaited him.

"And," Margo repeated dramatically, "the corporation is a blind one, set up by one Amanda Leigh McCloud."

The name pierced Jesse's heart. "Mandy?" he whispered in disbelief.

"Yes, Mandy," Margo confirmed, pursing her lips in distaste.

Jesse shook his head, refusing to believe her. "No. You're wrong. Mandy has no need for the Circle Bar. She's got all she can handle with the Double-Cross."

"That may well be true, but it *is* Mandy who instructed her lawyers to create the corporation and to make the offer. I have the proof."

"But why? Why would she go to the trouble of establishing a corporation just to buy the Circle Bar? Why wouldn't she just ask me outright?"

"I think that's obvious, don't you?" Margo folded her arms across her chest. "She didn't want you or anyone else to be privy to her plans until it was too late to do anything about it. She's a McCloud, after all, and the McClouds would do anything to get their hands on the Circle Bar.''

Pain swirled through Jesse's head. He dropped his head between his hands, the papers he still held scraping against his scalp. Mandy wouldn't do this, he told himself. Hell, she loved him! And she wouldn't sneak behind his back to try to buy the Circle Bar from him. She didn't need to. They were going to get married just as soon as Mandy felt Jaime could handle the news. Why buy the Circle Bar when it would be hers once they married?

Margo stepped from behind the desk and plucked the contract from Jesse's stiff fingers. ''She's played you for a fool, Jesse. Again,'' she added spitefully.

Jesse jerked his head up to glare at her. ''What is that supposed to mean?''

''She used you before to spite her father, and now she's using you again to wield her revenge on the Barristers.''

A muscle flexed on Jesse's jaw. ''That's not true.''

Margo arched a knowing brow. ''Isn't it? You know how badly Mandy and her sisters resented their father and his dominance in their lives. You were her one sure way to rebel against Lucas, to prove that he couldn't control her.'' Margo carefully refolded the papers, smoothing them between her fingers. ''The child may have been a part of her plan, or maybe an accident, I'm not sure.''

At Jesse's surprised look, a small smile of satisfaction curved Margo's lips. ''You weren't aware that I knew, were you?''

''But how—?''

Margo's smile quickly disappeared. "One only has to look at the boy to see the resemblance, both to you and to Wade." She tapped the thick document against her palm. "Others might be blind, but I never was," she said, her eyes narrowing dangerously. "I knew from the first time I saw him that he was yours, no matter what lies the McClouds spread to explain his existence."

Jesse hauled in a steadying breath. Lies, all of it, he told himself fiercely. Margo was making all this up. Mandy had never used him—she loved him, just as he loved her, and always had. "And what exactly do you think she's using me for this time?" he asked tersely.

Margo cocked her head to look at him in surprise. "Why, I'd think that is obvious. Mandy is and always will be a McCloud, and the McClouds have always hated the Barristers. To own the Circle Bar, to steal from right beneath the Barristers' very noses the land that they've worked for and struggled for all these years, would be, in their eyes, delivering the final comeuppance."

Margo looked down on Jesse, unable to hide her disgust. "You're just like your father. An easy mark for an ambitious woman. That McCloud girl kept you so busy panting after her that you didn't pay attention to business. That was a mistake, one that you'll pay for, and keep paying for, if you're not careful."

Jesse rose, unable to listen to any more. He snatched the contract from her hands and stuffed it into the rear pocket of his jeans. Then he turned and headed for the door.

"Where are you going?" Margo shrieked from behind him.

Jesse stopped, bracing his hands against the door

frame to keep from crumpling to his knees. "I'm going to the Double-Cross and talk to Mandy."

"The Double-Cross!" Margo tossed back her head and laughed, the chilling sound echoing shrilly around the room. "Fitting name, wouldn't you say, considering their underhanded scheme to purchase the Circle Bar?"

Jesse sucked in a sharp breath, steeling himself against the doubts Margo had managed to fill his mind with. He needed to talk to Mandy, he told himself. He needed to hear from her own lips that everything Margo had revealed was lies. Pushing off the door frame, he stormed from Wade's office without looking back.

Eight

Mandy sat at her desk, her boots propped on its polished surface, the phone receiver tucked between shoulder and ear. "It's hard to believe, isn't it? After all these years..." Her voice drifted off, ending on a dreamy sigh.

"Take copious notes. Maybe our writers can use this in upcoming scripts."

Mandy chuckled at the derisive tone in Merideth's voice. "It does rather sound like a soap-opera plot, doesn't it?"

"I suppose, though I personally wouldn't want to star in it. I've had my fill of cowboys and rural America. Give me New York any day of the year."

Laughing, Mandy rocked her chair back and lowered her boots to the floor. "I'll remind you of that come January, when you're freezing your buns off and wading through a foot of snow."

"I'd much rather wade through snow than cow manure."

Mandy could almost see the imperious lift of Merideth's chin. Her sister had always hated the ranch, while Mandy and Sam had loved it. Just one of many differences between the sisters that made each unique. But in spite of their dissimilarities, their love for each other was solid. Each one of them would do anything to help the others, which made Mandy ask, "When are you coming home again for another visit?"

"Heavens!" Merideth exclaimed. "I was just there!"

"I know," Mandy replied, smiling self-consciously. "But I want you to meet Jesse."

"I've met Jesse," Merideth reminded her dryly.

"I know, but that was years ago. I want you to see him now. Get to know him."

"So that I can place my stamp of approval on him before my big sister marries him and rides off into the sunset to live happily ever after?"

Mandy rolled her eyes. "You're a brat, Merideth."

A sultry laugh flowed through the line to warm Mandy's ear and her heart. "Yeah, I know."

"You will come, won't you?"

"You know I will. Just as soon as I can arrange it. But I've got to run now. I've got this publicity thingy scheduled for three and I have to change into something sexy that screams wealth and success."

The breath Mandy had been holding bubbled out on a soft laugh at her sister's outrageousness. "Thanks, Merideth. I'll talk to you soon." She leaned forward to replace the receiver and heard the back door slam. "Jaime?" she called. "Is that you?" She rose, intending to send her son straight to the shower for a much-needed washing.

But she was surprised to hear Jesse's answering call. "No, it's me."

The tightness in his voice made Mandy's smile of greeting fade just a bit. It faded even more when he stepped into her office and she saw the angry scowl contorting his face. "Is something wrong?" she asked.

"Where's Jaime?"

"He's with Gabe. He was driving everybody crazy, waiting for you to return, so I sent him with Gabe to look for some lost calves." She took a step to round the desk, but stopped when Jesse jerked a wad of papers from his back pocket and threw them on the desk in front of her. Her gaze rose from the papers to his angry brown eyes. "Jesse, you're frightening me. What's wrong?"

He pointed a stiff finger at the offending document. "Do you know anything about this?"

Slowly, Mandy reached for the papers, wondering what in the world had come over Jesse. Sinking down onto her chair, she smoothed a palm across the creases, flattening the document on the top of her desk. The names Brickle & Stanton, Attorneys at Law, printed boldly across the top of the first page, fairly leaped from the paper to slap her. Her heart plummeted to her stomach, draining the blood from her face. "Oh, my God," she murmured.

"You know about this, then?"

The accusation in his voice frightened Mandy as much as the anger that she saw darkening his eyes when she found the courage to look up at him. "Yes."

Jesse's fist came down on the desk so hard the phone receiver rattled on its base. "Why didn't you tell me?

Why didn't you just *ask* me to sell you the Circle Bar? Why did you have to go behind my back?''

Mandy rose, realizing that Jesse considered this all some kind of devious plot against him personally. ''I forgot.''

As soon as the words were out of her mouth, she realized how foolish and inadequate they sounded.

''Forgot!'' Jesse echoed incredulously. ''How in the hell does a woman *forget* that she's put millions of dollars on the line for the purchase of land?''

His rage brought Mandy's own temper bubbling to the surface. ''It was easy,'' she returned furiously. ''First you showed up with Jaime in tow, determined to claim him as your son. *That* was certainly distraction enough. My son's safety was a great deal more important to me than the purchase of any land. Then you were here every day, a constant reminder of everything I thought I'd lost. Then—'' her voice broke and she had to stop and haul in a deep, steadying breath before she could go on. ''Then we became lovers again. Whether you care to believe me or not, with all that going on, the purchase of the Circle Bar was the *last* thing on my mind.''

Jesse wanted to believe her. Needed to. But Margo had done an excellent job of clouding his judgment with all her allegations.

''You used me, didn't you?'' he accused as he rounded the desk. ''First to rebel against Lucas, then to distract me so that I wouldn't know that you were the one who wanted to purchase the Circle Bar.''

With him so close, Mandy was forced to look up at him. ''No,'' she whispered. ''I never used you.'' She grabbed for his arms, sinking her fingers into the flesh there, hoping, needing to make him understand. ''I love you, Jesse. I always have. I didn't want the Circle Bar for me. I wanted it for Jaime. I couldn't give him his father, but I wanted him to have a part of his heritage, something the circumstances of his birth denied him.

"I didn't even know Wade had left you the ranch," she rushed to explain. "I assumed Margo inherited everything. And I knew she would never sell the place to a McCloud. So I had my lawyers form the corporation to conceal my identity from her."

The look he gave her was filled with contempt. "If that's the case, then why are the contracts made out to *me* as owner of the Circle Bar?"

"I knew nothing about the contract's existence until just now, when you tossed it on my desk."

Jesse's mouth curled in a sneer. "Yeah, right."

Her eyes widened. "It's true. I swear. My lawyer didn't tell me of the offer. There was no need to, since I gave him power of attorney to act on my behalf." She dug her nails deeper into his arms, desperate to make him understand. "I wouldn't ever do anything to hurt you, Jesse, or to deceive you. You've got to believe me."

Jesse felt her nails biting through his skin. But the pain was nothing compared to that which tore through his heart as he looked down into the face of the woman he loved, the woman he'd trusted.

Did he dare believe her? Oh, God, how he wanted to, but there was so much evidence stacked against her. He'd believed her once, believed her words of love, her pledge of a future with him.

I'm sorry, Jesse. I can't.

The despised memory of her last words to him on that night long ago returned to haunt him once again.

Grabbing her hands, he tore them from their hold on

him. "I want my son, Mandy. And I want him now. He can have the Circle Bar, but it'll be *me* giving it to him. Jesse Barrister. Not a McCloud."

Jaime ducked from the open doorway of his mother's office and pressed his back against the wall, swallowing hard.

My son? Was that what Jesse had called him?

He swallowed again, listening to the raised voices still coming from inside the office.

"I'm his father," he heard Jesse roar. "And I have every right to claim him as my own, and nothing you do or say will stop me this time from telling him the truth."

Jesse was his father?

Tears spurted to his eyes. But he couldn't be! Jaime cried silently. His father was dead. His mother had told him so herself, and his mother never lied.

Pushing himself from the wall, Jaime ran for his room, his exit, as well as his arrival, hidden from those in the office by the hallway's thick carpet.

Once inside the sanctuary of his room, he closed the door and pressed his back against it.

No! He can't be. He's not my father!

Angrily, he pushed from the door and crossed to stand in front of his dresser. He leaned close, staring hard at his reflection in the mirror, taking in each feature of his face. The cleft in his chin, the color of his skin. Even the cowlick in the middle of his forehead that refused to stay down no matter how much mousse he slathered on it. He took each feature and mentally matched it to those on Jesse's face.

Dragging in a deep breath, he took a disbelieving

step back, staring at what he now recognized as the truth.

Jaime McCloud was Jesse Barrister's son.

"Mandy!" Sam slammed the back door and took two steps into the kitchen before she stopped, grimacing. Glancing down at her mud-caked boots, she muttered a guilty "oops" then toed off first one boot, then the other. "Mandy!" she called again, kicking her boots in the general direction of the door. "Is anybody home?"

"I'm back here," came Mandy's muffled reply.

Grabbing a banana from the bowl of fruit on the kitchen counter, Sam headed for the office, peeling it. "Hey, I thought it was your turn to cook supper," she complained as she made the turn into the office. "I'm starving."

Mandy lifted her head from the desk, revealing red-rimmed eyes and tearstained cheeks. Sam's hand froze with the banana halfway to her mouth. "What's wrong?" she asked as she dropped the banana to the floor and ran to drop down at Mandy's side. "Has something happened to Jaime?"

Mandy shook her head, pressing a palm against her fevered brow. "No. I-it's Jesse. H-he—" Fresh sobs erupted and she dragged her hand down her face to clamp it over her mouth.

"Mandy!" Sam exclaimed in frustration. "Tell me what's happened!"

"J-Jesse found out about m-my offer to buy the Circle B-Bar," she stammered tearfully.

Sam sank from her squatting position to her knees. "Oh, my gosh. I forgot all about that," she murmured. "So d-did I," Mandy sobbed brokenly. "Not that

Jesse b-believes me. He's f-furious. He thinks I was u-using him so that the McClouds could g-gain control of the Circle Bar.''

Sam's eyes bugged wide. "He what?"

Mandy swiped a hand beneath her eyes. "I know. It s-sounds crazy, but that's w-what he believes."

Sam pushed to her feet, her cheeks flushed with anger. "Where is he? I'll set him straight."

"I don't know. He left in a rage." She dragged her sleeve beneath her nose. "But he'll be back. He swore that he's going to tell Jaime that he's his father whether I agree with him or not."

Sam firmed her lips. "Well, he'll have to get through me first."

Mandy rose, catching Sam's sleeve between her fingertips. "No, Sam. I think he's right. It's time Jaime knew the truth."

After washing her face, Mandy went to the kitchen to start dinner. Needing the sense of normalcy, leaning heavily on it, she peeled potatoes at the sink, trying not to think of Jesse and the accusations he'd hurled at her. Through the kitchen window she caught a glimpse of Gabe, climbing into his truck.

Where is he off to? she wondered, then froze. *Jaime!* He was supposed to be with Gabe! Dropping the paring knife and the potato to the sink, she ran for the back door, palming the screen open.

"Gabe!" she called. "Gabe! Wait up!"

Gabe slowed his truck, coming to a stop. Leaning across the seat, he ducked his head to peer at her through the open window on the passenger side. "Whatcha need, Mandy?"

Reaching the truck, Mandy closed her hands over

the window brace. "Where's Jaime?" she asked breathlessly.

Gabe frowned. "I thought he was at the house with you."

"No!" Mandy cried. "He was with you, looking for the lost calves."

"Yeah, but we've been back over an hour. Sent him to the house soon as we returned, just like you told me."

"But he didn't come back!" Mandy wailed.

"Are you sure?"

"Of course I am! I—" Then she stopped, her face going pale. "Stay right here," she ordered Gabe. "I'll be right back."

Jerking the screen door open again, she ran through the house, yelling Jaime's name. She flew past her office and came to a stop at the door to Jaime's room. Pressing a hand against her heart, praying that she'd find Jaime fast asleep on his bed, she opened the door, swung it wide. The bed was empty, as was the room. With her legs trembling, Mandy stepped inside.

The backpack that always hung on the end post of his bed was gone. Quickly, Mandy whirled—and bumped into Sam.

Sam caught her sister's arms, holding her in place, recognizing the fear in Mandy's eyes. "What's wrong?"

Mandy twisted from her arms. "Jaime's gone!" she cried, rushing past her.

"Gone?" Sam chased her down the hall. "Gone where?"

"I don't know," Mandy yelled as she shoved the screen open.

She ran for Gabe's truck. "He's not in the house,"

she gasped, fear tightening her chest. "Check the barn. See if his horse is there, then report back to me."

"Where could he've gone?" Gabe asked, concern deepening the creases at the corners of his eyes.

Mandy pushed away from the truck. "I don't know. But I'm calling Jesse."

Turning, she ran for the house again. Sam waited for her in the kitchen. "Would you please tell me what's going on?"

Mandy brushed past her and grabbed for the phone. She quickly punched in numbers, then raked her fingers through her hair, pulling painfully at the roots as she listened to first one frustrating ring, then another, and yet another. Slamming down the receiver, breaking the connection, she immediately grabbed it back up and punched in another series of numbers. She waited, holding her breath.

"Margo Barrister speaking."

Mandy's skin crawled at the sound of the woman's cool southern drawl, remembering another time she'd been forced to call Margo Barrister, looking for Jesse. "This is Mandy McCloud. I need to speak to Jesse."

"I'm sorry, he isn't here."

"Do you know when he'll return or how I can reach him?"

"Unfortunately, I don't. He was here less than an hour ago and packed his things and left without sharing his plans with me."

Icy dread filled Mandy's veins. Had Jesse disappeared again, taking Jaime with him? "Thank you," she murmured and replaced the receiver.

"Would you *please* tell me what's going on?" Sam demanded angrily.

"Jesse's gone, too. Margo said he packed his things and left less than an hour ago."

Sam's eyes widened. "You don't think——"

Mandy dug her fingers through her hair, trying to hold on to reason. "I don't know what to think," she murmured miserably.

The back door opened and Mandy jerked her head up just as Gabe stepped inside.

"His horse is gone," he said, scraping off his hat. "The sorrel mare. Not the paint Jesse gave him."

Mandy's breath whooshed out of her in relief. If his horse was gone, that meant that more than likely Jaime was on his own and not with Jesse. *But why?* she wondered frantically. *Why would he run away? Was it possible that he had overheard her and Jesse's argument in the office?*

The very idea had her knees weakening. It doesn't matter, she told herself firmly. The important thing was to find him. "Saddle my horse, Gabe. I'm going after him."

Gabe's forehead plowed into a frown. "It's gonna be dark soon. Why don't you stay here and let the boys and me search for him?"

Mandy lifted her chin, meeting his worried look with one of defiance. "No. He's my son. I'm going, too." Quickly she sketched out a plan. "Tell the men to mount up and y'all search the hills that lie between the Double-Cross and the Carters' ranch. I'll take the section that leads to the Circle Bar."

Gabe ducked his head, hiding his disapproval of her going out on her own. "Your horse'll be ready when you are." Turning, he clamped his battered hat on his head and disappeared through the back door.

"I'm going with you."

Mandy wagged her head. "No, Sam. Stay here. He might come home and I need you to be here for him."

Though Mandy could see that the idea of staying behind didn't appeal to Sam, she was relieved when Sam finally gave her head a quick nod. "Okay. But be careful, Mandy."

She grabbed Sam's hand and squeezed. "I will. And if Jaime should show up before I get back, don't let Jesse anywhere near him until I return."

Dusk was already turning the landscape into gloomy shadows by the time Mandy started out on her search. Looking for tracks was impossible, what with the number of horses that roamed the pastures every day. She racked her brain, frantically trying to think like Jaime.

Where would he have gone? Where would he go to hide?

But no clue to his location came to mind. Squeezing her thighs against the horse's sides, she urged him into a trot, calling Jaime's name over and over again as she traversed the pastures and hills, until her voice was hoarse, her throat raw. Until stars peppered the sky.

She fought back a sob, knowing the dangers that night brought in this rugged terrain. "Jaime. My baby," she whispered tearfully. "Where are you?"

Jesse drove north on I-35, headed for Oklahoma and home, his gaze riveted on the road ahead. He knew some would accuse him of running again, but it didn't matter. He wasn't running. Not this time. He was merely giving himself some time to think rationally without the distraction of Mandy's presence or the vindictiveness of Margo's tongue to influence him.

She's played you for a fool, Jesse. Again.

A fool. A fool. A fool.

Margo's words picked up the cadence of his truck's tires on the highway and pounded through his head.

With each mile the throbbing in his temples increased, until the pain nearly blinded him.

But it was nothing compared to the pain that vised his heart.

Mandy. He was leaving her behind again. And Jaime. His son. The child that he'd known nothing about until Wade's will had brought him back to Texas and the Circle Bar. He was leaving him behind, as well.

One only has to look at the boy to see the resemblance, both to you and to Wade. Others might be blind, but I never was. I knew from the first time I saw him that he was yours, no matter what lies the Mc-Clouds spread to explain his existence.

Like Margo, Jesse would have known Jaime was his son, too.

If he'd stayed all those years ago.

But he'd run, leaving behind the memories, leaving behind the woman who'd promised love and forever, unable to bear the anguish of losing Mandy.

He slapped a hand against the wheel. "Damn it! It wasn't just promises." Mandy *had* loved him. She still did. In his heart, he knew she'd never lied to him. Not then, and certainly not now.

Then why are you running away again?

Jesse narrowed an eye at the road ahead. "I'm not," he muttered under his breath, and jerked the wheel to the right, taking the exit to Georgetown. Crossing the overpass, he headed back down I-35. This time to the south. Back to Austin. Back to Mandy. Back to the son he yearned to claim as his own.

He didn't stop until he reached the Double-Cross.

Parking at the rear of the house, he stormed to the back door. Before he even reached the steps, the door was opening. But it was Sam, not Mandy, who stood in the wedge of light cast from the kitchen behind her. By her expression, he could only assume that he was no longer welcome on the Double-Cross.

"Where's Mandy?"

Sam's lips thinned and she planted her hands defiantly on her hips. "Haven't you hurt her enough?"

"I need to talk to her."

"From what I heard, I think you've said all she's willing to listen to."

"Sam, please." Jesse dragged off his hat and dropped his head, digging his fingers through his hair.

Sam saw the slight tremble in his fingers, but it was when he lifted his head and she saw the tears in his eyes that she felt her resolve weakening.

"I love her, Sam. I need to tell her that."

Sam wavered only a second before she blurted out, "Jaime ran away."

Jesse's fingers closed around his hat's brim, crushing it between his hands. "When?"

Sam's shoulders drooped, losing their defensive stance as worry burned through. "I don't know. Mandy left on horseback about an hour ago to search for him."

"I need a horse."

Sam prayed that Mandy would forgive her. "You can take mine. First stall on the left."

Jesse wheeled, then turned back. "Thank you, Sam. I owe you one."

Within minutes, Jesse had Sam's horse and was loping across the pasture, the moon and stars offering the only illumination against the dark night. Mandy had an hour lead on him, but he was determined to catch up with her before she found Jaime. He wanted to be there when they found him, and they *would* find him. He wouldn't allow himself to consider any other possibility.

He rode through the night, watching and listening, his fear for his son growing with each passing minute. Then a sound, muffled by the stand of trees he was passing through, made him pull his horse up short. He stood up in the stirrups, straining to listen.

"Jaime!"

The sound of Mandy's voice coming from just ahead of him had him digging his heels into the roan's sides. He galloped toward the sound, mindless of the scrape of tree branches that slapped at his arms and face.

When the trees thinned, he saw her, standing on a ledge of rock, her hands cupped to her mouth, her horse ground-tethered not too far behind her.

"Mandy!" he yelled. "Mandy!"

She turned, spotlighted by moonlight, to stare at him. The defeat in her eyes frightened him as much or more than hearing of Jaime's disappearance. He reined his horse to an abrupt stop and swung down from the saddle.

"I can't find him," she murmured dismally. "I've looked everywhere. The places where he usually camps out, his favorite fishing holes."

"Oh, Mandy." Jesse wrapped her in his arms and drew her close. "We'll find him. I promise we'll find him."

"It's so dark," she cried, curling her fingers into his shirt. "What if he's lying hurt somewhere?"

"Jaime's not some greenhorn, Mandy. He knows how to handle himself out in the wild."

"But where is he?" she demanded hysterically.

"Have you looked on the Circle Bar?"

Mandy pushed from his arms to look at him, her tear-filled eyes wide. "No, he would never—"

Jesse caught her hand, leading her back to her horse. "There's a cave there," he told her, picking his way carefully through the loose rocks and cacti that covered the ground near the ledge. "When I was a boy, I used to hide out there myself. If I know Jaime, I'll bet he discovered that cave long ago."

With Jesse taking the lead, they remounted and pressed on, heading for Circle Bar land. They rode for what seemed like hours to Mandy, before Jesse pulled up, holding up his hand. He jumped down from his horse, then turned to Mandy. "We'd better walk the rest of the way. It's too dangerous to try to navigate the path at night."

After tethering their horses to a tree, Jesse caught her hand, pulling her along behind him. He stopped suddenly and Mandy bumped into him. "What?" she asked anxiously.

Jesse pressed a finger to her lips, then pointed. Jaime's horse grazed on a patch of grass to their left. "He's here," he whispered, then tightened his hold on her hand, pulling her after him.

Cedar choked the entrance to the cave, but Jesse knew it was there. He pushed branches aside until he found the jagged opening, then held them back for Mandy to enter in front of him. She stepped inside and stopped, unable to see so much as the hand in front of her face through the inky blackness.

"I can't see," she whispered.

Jesse stepped around her. "Here. I've got a lighter." His thumb scraped the wheel, and a small flame burst forth, offering a soft circle of light. Jesse took another step, then another with Mandy pressed at his back. He stopped, holding the lighter high. In its glow, he saw the sleeping bag and the huddled form wrapped in it. A small gasp escaped Mandy and she pushed past Jesse while he stooped to light the kerosene lantern that Jaime had left beside his bedroll.

"Jaime," she murmured, dropping to her knees at her son's side. "Oh, Jaime."

He lifted his head, blinking. "Mama?" he asked, his voice rough with sleep.

"Yes, Jaime. It's Mama." She ran a hand over his cheek, just to prove to herself that he wasn't hurt. "Oh, sweetheart, why did you run away?"

Jaime pushed himself to a sitting position, shrinking away from her touch. "You lied to me. You said that my father was dead."

Regret clogged Mandy's throat as she realized he had in fact overheard her conversation with Jesse. "Yes, Jaime," she admitted softly. "I lied. But I didn't do it to hurt you. Only to protect you."

Jesse moved closer, unsure what his level of participation should be, and set the lamp beside his foot as he hunkered down beside Mandy. He lifted a hand to her shoulder and squeezed.

Jaime's gaze shot to him. "You're my father, aren't you?"

Mandy glanced up to meet Jesse's gaze. His questioning. Hers reassuring. "It's okay," she murmured. "He needs to know the truth."

Sighing, Jesse turned to face his son. "Yes, Jaime. I'm your father."

Jaime flattened his hands on his bedroll and dug in

his heels, scooting back, putting distance between them. "I hate you!" he screamed wildly.

Mandy sucked in a shocked breath. "Jaime! You don't mean that!"

"Yes I do!" he cried, turning on Jesse. "You only pretended to like me. If you really cared for me, for my mom, you would've been here before, when we needed you." He hauled in a shuddery breath. "We don't want you here. Go back where you came from and leave us alone."

The knife that had wedged itself in Jesse's heart when Jaime had first screamed "I hate you," twisted in his chest. Pressing his hands to his knees, he rose, emotion burning his throat as he turned away.

Mandy grabbed his hand, stopping him. "No! Wait!" Clinging to Jesse, Mandy turned to face their son. "He does care for you, Jaime. It isn't Jesse's fault that he wasn't there when you were born."

Jaime's scowl deepened. "Yes, it is. If he cared, he'd have been there. He wouldn't have let Grandpa treat you so mean."

Mandy's eyes widened in surprise. "You were only a baby when Grandpa died. You couldn't possibly know how he treated me."

Jaime's mouth curled into a belligerent pout. "Yes, I do. I've heard you and Aunt Sam and Aunt Merideth talkin' when y'all thought I wasn't around. I know that he didn't want me and he hated you for bringing me to the Double-Cross to live."

Instinctively, Mandy reached for him, but Jaime drew back, refusing her comfort. Tears clotted in Mandy's throat as she drew her hands into an empty fist on her lap. "Oh, Jaime, I'm so sorry. I never wanted you to know all of that." She dipped her chin, drawing a deep breath before she lifted her gaze to Jaime's again. "But it wasn't your fault that Grandpa didn't want us around. And it wasn't mine, either. It was Grandpa's.

"Do you remember when Jesse was talking to you about prejudices?" Though she could tell he resented her bringing Jesse's name into the discussion, Mandy pressed on. "Well, Grandpa was like that. He didn't like Jesse. First because he was a Barrister, and second because he was part-Mexican." She peered closely at Jaime. "Do you think that was fair of Grandpa, to hold those two things against him?"

Unable to meet her gaze any longer, Jaime ducked his head, plucking at fuzz balls on his sleeping bag. "No," he muttered.

Mandy released a long, slow breath. "I didn't, either. So I defied my father when he refused to let me see Jesse. I slipped out at night and met him in secret." She glanced up at Jesse and caught his hand again, drawing him back down beside her. "I did that because I loved Jesse. I wanted to marry him. But my father caught us one night and he threatened to kill Jesse if I ever saw him again.

"And I was afraid. More afraid than I'd ever been in my life, because I was sure that my father would make good on that threat. So I refused to leave with Jesse, choosing instead to stay with my father." She shifted her gaze to Jesse's. "But I only did that so that I could buy some time in order to figure out a way for Jesse and me to be together always."

Squeezing Jesse's hand, she turned her gaze back to Jaime. "But Jesse didn't understand what I was trying to do. He thought I was choosing my father over him. He left that night, not knowing that I already carried you, and moved away, not telling anyone where he was going. I didn't see him again until that day when he brought you back to the Double-Cross after he'd caught you fishing on Barrister land. He never knew you existed until that day.''

Throughout her explanation, Jaime had sat rigidly, listening, but when she paused, he turned his gaze on Jesse again, his expression still hostile, unforgiving. "How did you know I was your son?''

Knowing how important this was, how much of his future depended on his response, Jesse chose his words carefully. ''I didn't at first, but when you told me your name was McCloud, I started putting it all together. You looked like me. Your age, as best as I could tell, seemed about right.'' Jesse lifted a shoulder.

Jaime's thin chest swelled beneath his T-shirt. "Then why didn't you tell *me?*'' he shouted, balling his hand in his tangled bedroll.

''I—''

Mandy put a hand on Jesse's arm to interrupt him. "He wanted to,'' she said softly. "But I wouldn't let him.''

''Why not?'' Jaime demanded angrily. ''I had a right to know who my real dad was!''

''Yes,'' Mandy replied patiently, ''you did. But I was afraid that the news would be too hard for you to accept. You didn't even know Jesse. He was a stranger to you. I thought that if you and Jesse had a chance to get to know each other first, that the news would be easier for you to accept.''

''I'm not a baby. I would've understood.''

Mandy reached for his hand and this time Jaime let her take it. "I can see that now, although it's very hard for me to admit that my son's growing up. I guess in some ways I'll always consider you my baby.''

Jaime rolled his eyes. ''Oh, geez, Mom, don't get all sappy on me.''

Mandy laughed in spite of the tears that pooled in her eyes. ''I'll try not to, I promise.'' She looked up at Jesse, knowing that all was not settled yet. ''Jesse wanted to tell you you were his son from the first moment that he saw you and I'm sorry that I stood in his way.''

Jaime shifted his gaze to Jesse, looking for confirmation.

''It's true, son,'' Jesse murmured, his own throat tight with emotion. ''I may not have been around when you were born, but that doesn't mean that I don't love you or want you. I do, and I want to claim you as my own. In fact—'' he glanced at Mandy, needing her approval before looking back at his son ''—I'd like to give you my name. I can adopt you, if the law requires it, and we can change your name to Jaime Barrister.''

Beside him, Mandy rocked back on her heels, her eyes wide with shock. ''Barrister!'' she cried on a disbelieving breath. The name had been like a curse word in her family's home for so many years, hearing it coupled with her son's name was like blasphemy.

Jesse squared his shoulders defensively. ''I may not be proud of the man who gave me the name, but the name is mine.''

Seeing that she'd insulted him, Mandy reached for his hand. ''I'm sorry. It's just that...''

Jesse took her hand more firmly in his and squeezed. ''I know,'' he said, understanding her initial reaction. ''But I think it's well past time we put that old feud to rest, don't you?''

"Well, y-yes," Mandy stammered. "I guess it is."

Jesse turned his attention back to his son. "I'm not ashamed of you, I want you to know that, and I'll be proud to tell the world that you're my son. I know that having a father is going to take some getting used to, but I hope you'll give me the chance to prove that I truly love you." He shifted his gaze to Mandy's, his expression softening, though his words were for his son. "I love your mother, too. Always have. And if it's okay with you, I'd like to ask her to marry me."

Because he'd wanted the same thing ever since he'd met Jesse, Jaime grinned. "I guess that'd be all right."

"Mandy?"

Mandy stared at Jesse, her heart in her throat, unable to believe this was all really happening. "Yes?"

"Will you marry me?"

It took Mandy less than a second to make the decision. She fell into his waiting arms, laughing and crying. "Yes, I'll marry you!" she cried.

Drawing her closer against his chest, Jesse dropped his head over hers, finding her lips.

"Oh, gross!" Jaime exclaimed, making a gagging sound. "Cut it out, you two, or I'm gonna hurl for sure."

Drawing apart, Jesse and Mandy met each other's gaze, laughing. They stared a moment, their expressions slowly sobering, both aware of how far they'd come and how much farther they still had to go before the past could be fully resolved.

"Barrister," Mandy murmured, staring deeply into Jesse's dark eyes. "Mandy McCloud Barrister." A laugh bubbled up from her throat. "I wonder what the

McClouds and the Barristers, both past and present, will think about that?''

''To hell with them,'' Jesse whispered, pulling her into his arms again. ''It's what we want that matters. You, me and our son.''

Epilogue

"I think I'm going to cry."

Keeping her eyes on the bride and groom who stood behind a three-tier wedding cake, laughing as they fed each other generous bites of the white confection, Merideth slung an arm around Sam's slender shoulders and drew her sister to her side. "And ruin the makeup job I did on you? Don't even consider it."

Reminded of the hours of primping she'd suffered through prior to the wedding at Merideth's insistence, Sam grimaced and folded her arms beneath her breasts. "I feel like some kind of cheap floozy."

Merideth turned her head slowly, arching a haughty brow, as she looked down at her sister. "Cheap? Darling, I don't do cheap. First class, top of the line, that's my motto."

"Easy for you to say. You like painting your face." Scowling, Sam glanced down at the dress Merideth had brought her from New York and immediately caught the scooped neckline and hauled it higher up on her chest. "And this dress! Cripes! A handkerchief would've covered more."

Merideth dropped her arm from Sam's shoulder to give the dress a sharp tug down, drawing the bodice back into line. "If I left it up to you, you would have worn grubby jeans and manure-caked boots to our sister's wedding."

"I would've been a lot more comfortable, I assure you."

Merideth smiled while she turned her gaze on the wedding guests. "Yes, but just think of all the compliments you've received."

"Yeah. Right," Sam muttered wryly. "All delivered to my breasts."

Merideth laughed, the sound throaty and deep. Sam noticed that more than a few men glanced her sister's way, their eyes filled with a mixture of curiosity and longing. Sam was sure that the sultry smile Merideth gave each one would keep the men awake that night, thinking sinful thoughts while they lay beside their sleeping wives.

"For heaven's sake, Merideth. Cut it out," she complained.

"What?" Merideth asked innocently.

Sam rolled her eyes. "Turn off the charm before you give one of these poor guys a heart attack."

Merideth laughed again, tossing her hair over her shoulder. "A little harmless flirting. You should try it some time."

"No thanks." Sam glanced around, frowning. "Have you seen Jaime?"

"Not since I took a glass of champagne away from him."

Sam scanned the crowd. "I promised Mandy I would keep an eye on him. Oh, look," Sam said, her eyes brightening. "There's John Lee Carter. I didn't see him at the ceremony."

Merideth followed her sister's gaze, her heart stuttering a bit when she met John Lee's gaze. Eyes as blue as the Texas sky above seemed to bore right through her, stripping her of her clothes and laying her bare. Fighting the delicious thrill that shivered down her spine at his blatant perusal, she puckered her lips and blew him a teasing kiss before glancing away. Though tempting, John Lee was too much like Merideth for her to take his look seriously.

Shifting her attention back to the table where the bride and groom lifted crystal flutes of champagne in a silent toast, Merideth blanked John Lee Carter from her mind.

In spite of herself, she felt her heart melt a little at the look the newlyweds shared. "They were destined to be together," she said on a sigh.

"Yeah, they were."

"It's perfect, isn't it?" Merideth offered thoughtfully. "Jesse and Mandy are finally together. Jaime gets a dad, plus the heritage he so richly deserves. And the Circle Bar and the Double-Cross Heart ranches are one again, the way they were meant to be." Suddenly she tossed back her head and laughed.

"What?" Sam asked, eyeing her dubiously.

"I'll bet Daddy is rolling in his grave right now."

Sam bit back a grin as she turned her gaze back to the newlyweds. "Yeah, and I'd wager Wade's probably doing some rolling of his own." Her grin softened into a wistful smile as she watched Jesse pull Mandy into his arms for a kiss. He withdrew slightly and whispered something to Mandy which had her smiling and linking her arm through his. Sam watched them walk away.

"Wonder where they're going?" she asked curiously.

Mandy had walked this path many times over the years, but seldom in the light of day, and never with Jesse at her side. She squeezed Jesse's arm as they stepped from the shadow of the trees and into the sunlit glen.

"This is where I came when I needed to feel near you," she whispered as she let her gaze wander over what had once been their secret meeting place.

Slipping his arm from hers, Jesse draped it across her shoulders and pulled her close against his side. "I wish I had been here for you."

Hearing the regret in his voice, Mandy turned to face him, looping her arms around his waist and smiling as she looked up into his eyes. "Oh, but you were. Always. I would come here and talk to you, tell you my fears, share with you my joys. I always felt your presence, your comfort, even though I had no idea where you were."

Sighing, Jesse hugged her to him, his heart full to near bursting with his love for her. "Oh, Mandy," he whispered. "We lost so many years, so much—"

She leaned back and pressed a finger to his lips, silencing him. "We have today and tomorrow and always. We aren't going to think about the past, only our future."

Jesse caught her hand in his and kissed her fingers,

then smiled as he drew her hand to his heart. "I am one lucky man."

The beat of his heart beneath her palm, the heat of his flesh blending with her own, brought back memories to Mandy of other times they had stood just so in this glen. "Jesse?" she began hesitantly.

"Yes, *querida?*"

"I know that you wanted to go some place special for our honeymoon night, and I really appreciate the thought, but would you mind if we…"

Jesse frowned, wondering at her hesitancy. "Mind if we what?"

Mandy felt her cheeks heat in embarrassment and dipped her chin, unable to meet his gaze. "Well, if it's all right with you, I'd really like to spend our first night as husband and wife here in the glen."

Jesse tossed back his head and laughed, then caught Mandy up in his arms and swung her around, his lips finding hers. "Oh, *querida.* My love. I can't think of a more perfect place to spend the night with you."

* * * * *

*Watch for Book #2 of Peggy Moreland's
exciting TEXAS BRIDES
series, THE RESTLESS VIRGIN, coming
in August 1998. In this emotional story,
Samantha McCloud falls in love for the
very first time. Don't miss it!*

THE TALLCHIEFS

the beloved miniseries by
USA Today bestselling author

Cait London

continues with
RAFE PALLADIN:
MAN OF SECRETS
(SD #1160)
Available August 1998

When takeover tycoon Rafe Palladin set out to *acquire* Demi Tallchief as part of a business deal, Demi had a few conditions of her own. And Rafe had some startling secrets to reveal....

"Cait London is one of the best writers in contemporary romance today."   —*Affaire de Coeur*

And coming from Desire in **December 1998,** look for **The Perfect Fit** in which *Man of the Month* Nick Palladin lures Ivory Tallchief back home to Amen Flats, Wyoming.

Available at your favorite retail outlet.

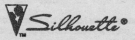

Take 2 bestselling love stories FREE

Plus get a FREE surprise gift!

Special Limited-Time Offer

Mail to Silhouette Reader Service™

3010 Walden Avenue
P.O. Box 1867
Buffalo, N.Y. 14240-1867

YES! Please send me 2 free Silhouette Desire® novels and my free surprise gift. Then send me 6 brand-new novels every month, which I will receive months before they appear in bookstores. Bill me at the low price of $3.12 each plus 25¢ delivery and applicable sales tax, if any.* That's the complete price, and a saving of over 10% off the cover prices—quite a bargain! I understand that accepting the books and gift places me under no obligation ever to buy any books. I can always return a shipment and cancel at any time. Even if I never buy another book from Silhouette, the 2 free books and the surprise gift are mine to keep forever.

225 SEN CH7U

Name	(PLEASE PRINT)	
Address		Apt. No.
City	State	Zip

This offer is limited to one order per household and not valid to present Silhouette Desire® subscribers. *Terms and prices are subject to change without notice.
Sales tax applicable in N.Y.

UDES-98 ©1990 Harlequin Enterprises Limited

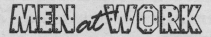

MEN at WORK

All work and no play? Not these men!

July 1998

MACKENZIE'S LADY by Dallas Schulze

Undercover agent Mackenzie Donahue's
lazy smile and deep blue eyes were his best
weapons. But after rescuing—and kissing!—
damsel in distress Holly Reynolds, how could
he betray her by spying on her brother?

August 1998

MISS LIZ'S PASSION by Sherryl Woods

Todd Lewis could put up a building with ease,
but quailed at the sight of a classroom! Still,
Liz Gentry, his son's teacher, was no battle-ax,
and soon Todd started planning some
extracurricular activities of his own....

September 1998

A CLASSIC ENCOUNTER by Emilie Richards

Doctor Chris Matthews was intelligent, sexy
and *very* good with his hands—which made
him all the more dangerous to single mom
Lizette St. Hilaire. So how long could she
resist Chris's special brand of TLC?

Available at your favorite retail outlet!

MEN AT WORK™

HARLEQUIN® ▼ *Silhouette®*

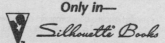

Catch more great

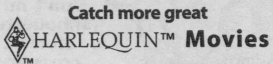 **HARLEQUIN™ Movies**

featured on

Premiering July 11th
Another Woman
Starring Justine Bateman and
Peter Outerbridge
Based on the novel by Margot Dalton

Don't miss next month's movie!
Premiering August 8th
The Waiting Game
Based on the novel by *New York Times*
bestselling author Jayne Ann Krentz

If you are not currently a subscriber to
The Movie Channel, simply call your
local cable or satellite provider for more
details. Call today, and don't miss out
on the romance!

    **HARLEQUIN®**
Makes any time special ™

100% pure movies.
100% pure fun.

MATERNITY LEAVE

Coming September 1998

Three delightful stories about the blessings
and surprises of "Labor" Day.

TABLOID BABY by Candace Camp

She was whisked to the hospital in the nick of time....

THE NINE-MONTH KNIGHT
by Cait London

A down-on-her-luck secretary is experiencing
odd little midnight cravings....

THE PATERNITY TEST by Sherryl Woods

The stick turned blue before her
biological clock struck twelve....

*These three special women are very pregnant...and very
single, although they won't be either for too much longer,
because baby—and Daddy—are on their way!*

Available at your favorite retail outlet.

The World's Most Eligible Bachelors are about
to be named! And Silhouette Books brings
them to you in an all-new, original series....

World's Most Eligible Bachelors

Twelve of the sexiest, most sought-after men share
every intimate detail of their lives in twelve never-
before-published novels by the genre's top authors.

Don't miss these unforgettable stories by:

Dixie Browning

Marie Ferrarella

Jackie Merritt

Tracy Sinclair

BJ James

Rachel Lee   Suzanne Carey

Gina Wilkins

VICTORIA PADE

Maggie Shayne   *Anne McAllister*

Susan Mallery

Look for one new book each month in the
World's Most Eligible Bachelors series beginning
September 1998 from Silhouette Books.

V™ *Silhouette®*

Available at your favorite retail outlet.